A LAWMAN'S REWARD

Love's a Gamble Book Three

KAY P. DAWSON

A Lawman's Reward

Print version

© Copyright 2022 (As Revised) Kay P. Dawson

CKN Christian Publishing
An Imprint of Wolfpack Publishing
5130 S. Fort Apache Rd. 215-380
Las Vegas, NV 89148

www.cknchristianpublishing.com

This book is a work of fiction. Any references to historical events, real people or real places are used fictitiously. Other names, characters, places and events are products of the author's imagination, and any resemblance to actual events, places or persons, living or dead, is entirely coincidental.

All rights reserved. No part of this book may be reproduced by any means without the prior written consent of the publisher, other than brief quotes for reviews.

Print ISBN 978-1-63977-209-4

A LAWMAN'S REWARD

CHAPTER 1

"Well, you're in luck. My dear husband and I run the Merchants Hotel right on the main street in Abilene. We have a room just for young teachers who are brave enough to try their hand at civilizing the children of this town. Your room is paid for by the parents who pay your wages. It's not much, but you have a roof over your head, a warm bed to sleep in, and meals prepared for you in the small restaurant downstairs."

Lydia couldn't believe her luck at riding the stagecoach with the proprietor of the hotel she'd be staying in. She hadn't sent word ahead to say she'd be coming back to Abilene yet, so her brother wouldn't know to meet her.

She smiled as she looked out the window and started to see some of the familiar sights of the small town that had grown up around her since she was a little girl. Abilene hadn't been much when they were kids and, in fact, had only started out as a stagecoach stop named Mud Creek when was about six. Over the years, the name had been changed to Abilene, and Kansas had since become a state.

At the time, she didn't really pay much attention to everything that was happening, other than she knew more people were moving to the area and the town was getting bigger. After spending the past few months at the Kansas Normal School getting her teacher's training, she'd learned more about the history of her area.

Abilene was now a bustling cow town and had become a bit rough around the edges with people passing through and causing trouble. The last teacher in town had run off within only a few weeks of taking the job. It wasn't a town that many women wanted to live in on their own.

But Lydia had grown up around here and everyone knew her brother, Brooks. At one time, he'd been a well-known gambler who'd had his own share of trouble until he'd found a woman to marry and settle down with. People still knew of his name around here and she knew people wouldn't want to mess with him, so she figured she'd be safer than most women might be.

Not to mention the fact that her brother's best friend was Lewis Kinkaid, one of the top lawmen of the town. She knew that since the town had become more wild with the drifters and cowboys passing through, there'd been many other lawmen who'd come and gone, working alongside Lewis. But he'd stayed, determined he wouldn't let the ruffians drive him away.

Her heart did a little flutter as her thoughts drifted to him. For as long as she'd known Lewis, she'd been attracted to him. His dark blond hair and the touch of stubble that always covered his strong jaw drew her eyes but truthfully, it was his kind and caring personality that had always appealed to her the most.

He was the kind of man you knew you could depend on.

But she wasn't foolish enough to believe a man like him would ever be interested in her, so she'd never let anyone know of her feelings.

She'd been living on the farm with her brother ever since their parents died many years ago and he'd looked after her. But once Brooks had fallen in love and married, she'd known she couldn't stay with the newlywed couple as they started their new life together. So she'd packed her bags to go to teacher's college, never believing she'd be coming back here to teach.

The creaking of the springs in the bouncy stagecoach filled the air as the dust settled around the people inside. It was late in the year but there was still some warmth in the sun as it peeked in through the windows. She could see the outline of the town in the distance and her whole body felt warm knowing she was back home. Soon, she'd see her brother and his wife Fiona who'd become one of her best friends.

Her heart was beating double time, though, because she also knew she'd soon be seeing the man she'd thought about every day since she'd left.

She jumped as the sound of the bugle alerted the station they were arriving. She gave a nervous laugh as she brought her hand up to her chest, smiling across at Mrs. Malloy. "Goodness, that startled me. I was deep in thought, I guess."

Mrs. Malloy patted her knee. "My Harold will be waiting and he can help you get your belongings moved over to the hotel. Oh, I can't tell you how happy I am, knowing you'll be staying with us. I will enjoy the company, that's for sure."

The stagecoach bounced into town and Lydia immediately saw the familiar sights of people milling everywhere she looked, horses riding down the street, dodging wagons that bumped through the ruts. She smiled to herself as she went past the sheriff's office and her breath caught in her throat when the man himself came out the front door, watching as the stagecoach made its way into town.

He was looking right at her, so she waved through the open window, wondering if he'd even see her. A smile lit up his face and as the stage moved past to head around the corner, he jumped down from the stairs, onto the street to follow them.

She tried to ignore the clenching of her stomach as her nerves caused everything, even her skin, to tingle. But he seemed happy to see her.

As the coach stopped with one last bounce forward, she patted at her skirts, trying to get some of the dust and wrinkles out from the trip here from the school in Emporia. The seats lurched forward, indicating the driver had stepped down and, within seconds, the door was being opened.

"Lydia Vaughn. I thought that was you but Brooks hadn't mentioned you'd be back in town yet. I thought for sure you'd taken off for greener and much more civilized pastures."

Lewis's smooth voice reached her ears and she smiled out as he reached in to take her hand and help her step outside.

"That's because I haven't told him. I thought I'd surprise him."

He still held her hand as he helped her step away from the stagecoach and up onto the wooden sidewalk. She was wearing gloves but she could feel the skin beneath the fabric warming from his touch.

"Let me get your bags and I'll take you out to the farm so you can surprise him."

"No, that's fine, Lewis. Thank you. I'm actually staying here in town at the Merchants Hotel. I'm the new teacher." She grinned at the shocked look on his face.

"Why would you come back to this rough and tumble town to teach when you could have gone anywhere else in the country?"

She gave a small laugh as she looked around, avoiding his gaze. If he saw the truth in her eyes, she'd be mortified.

"I figured this town needed someone used to the less civilized residents and happenings, so when I was told there was an opening here, I decided there's no better place than home."

She brought her eyes back up to his and smiled. "Besides, now that Brooks is married, I might just have some little ones to bounce on my knee soon. I wouldn't want to miss out on that. He's the only family I have left."

Lewis gave a loud laugh. "I feel for poor Fiona when that happens. She'll have two children to look after."

Lydia chuckled and gave him a gentle tap on the arm. "Lewis, you know Brooks doesn't act like a child...all the time." They both laughed at the familiar, inside joke.

"Well, I'll help you get your bags to the hotel then." He walked over to the driver and helped the man take the bags down. Lydia smiled as she watched him working.

"My, I've never known Mr. Kinkaid to be so

attentive to anyone. He's always been very kind, and I know he's well liked around here, but he sure seems happy to see you, my dear."

Mrs. Malloy gave her a wink, then turned to give the older man a hug who'd come up behind them. "Oh, Harold, I missed you terribly." She watched the couple embrace and felt a sadness as she wondered if she'd ever have that kind of love for herself.

When they were done, she pulled the man over to meet Lydia. "Harold, this young lady is Lydia Vaughn. She's been at teaching school in Emporia for the past few months but she's from right here in Abilene. She'd already left for school when we arrived to take over the hotel."

The man took Lydia's hand and smiled at her as he shook it.

"She's agreed to come back here and be the schoolteacher for our town, so she'll be staying with us."

"It's nice to meet you, ma'am. I look forward to having you stay with us." His eyes were kind and they held a twinkle that reminded Lydia of her father before her accident.

Shaking her head at the memory, she turned as Lewis came up with her bags. "I'll get Lydia's things over to the hotel, Harold. You look like you'll have your hands full with Edna's." Lewis nodded his head toward the pile of bags at Harold's feet, laughing as he led Lydia down the street toward the hotel.

"So, did you have fun staying in Emporia? I figured some young man would come along and sweep you off your feet and I'd be hearing you'd run off to get married."

She rolled her eyes in his direction. "It was fun and I did meet a lot of new people while I was there. But as for getting swept off my feet, I don't expect that to be happening any time soon." She looked down at the ground, hoping her limp wasn't too noticeable today. Riding in the stagecoach had aggravated it and she was feeling the stiffness.

Not wanting him to start feeling the pity she knew people felt when they noticed she had difficulty walking, she smiled up at him as he walked beside her. "How about you? Any ladies finally catch your eye?"

He huffed loudly and this time it was him rolling his eyes toward her. "You know I'm not really the settling down type."

Yes, she did know that. He'd made it clear for a long time he wasn't interested in chasing after any woman, even if she'd ever had the courage to let him know she was interested.

She was his friend's sister and not the type of woman to catch a man's eye. Especially not one like Lewis who'd already decided he'd never be tied to a woman.

CHAPTER 2

"I don't like it. It isn't safe in town but she won't listen to reason." Brooks banged his hand onto the desk, making Lewis look up at him with one eyebrow raised.

"Why don't you tell me how you're really feeling?"

"Well this town isn't safe for a woman alone. Trust me, I know." Lewis gave a little laugh to himself as Brooks continued, "I'm expecting you to keep an eye on her, you know."

Lewis leaned back in his chair, looping his fingers behind his head. "What if she doesn't want me keeping an eye on her? She's a big girl, Brooks. She can look after herself."

Of course, he wouldn't ever admit to his friend that he'd already been having the same worries about Lydia and had already planned to keep a close eye on her. He'd worked this town long enough to know how unruly and dangerous it was.

Lydia was an easy target for anyone wanting to take advantage of her too. Her kindness would be seen as weakness, so he was going to have to be extra diligent in keeping her safe. She'd been so excited yesterday when he'd walked her to her new hotel room, talking about how she was ready to teach the children in town and build a life of her own.

He'd offered to ride out to let Brooks and Fiona know she was home but she'd asked him to wait until morning. She said she knew Brooks was going to argue with her about her decision and she was tired after being stuck in the stagecoach all day.

They'd eaten their dinner together in the restaurant below the hotel while she shared stories from her time in Emporia. And he regaled her with tales from what had been going on around here.

As soon as he'd ridden out to tell her brother she was home this morning, Brooks had raced back to town behind him, determined to talk some sense into his sister. Lydia and Fiona had now just walked down to the mercantile, leaving Lewis to try calming Brooks down.

"Hopefully, after a few days of actually being right in the middle of town and seeing what all goes on around here, she'll come to her senses and come back to the farm. There's no reason I can't simply bring her in each day to the school if she's still determined to teach here."

"Brooks, you know as well as I do how much of a hassle that would be, especially during the months you need to be working the fields. It's coming up to winter here, so the men drifting through from the cattle drives will be slowing down. It'll mostly be locals and men passing through to work the stock-yards and rails. Hopefully, she'll be all settled in by the time spring comes around and things start to pick up around here again."

The Deputy US Marshal, Tom Smith walked in and went over to sit behind his desk. Since he'd arrived in town at the end of last year, he'd insisted he could run this town with no guns, relying only on his own hands and wit to look after the citizens. He believed Abilene had become too dangerous, so had banned guns within town limits.

He wasn't a popular man with the cowboys and drifters who passed through but he was tough and had proven he could look after the place. He'd had a couple of assassination attempts but survived, so Lewis admired how well he could handle himself.

"Tom, will you tell Brooks his sister, Lydia, will be safe staying in Abilene to teach at the school? "Lewis grinned at Brooks, knowing he'd never argue with a man like Tom "Bear River" Smith.

"I'll make sure Lewis keeps his eye on your sister and if he can't handle the duty, I'll find someone who can." This time it was Tom who grinned at Lewis, knowing how much he didn't like anyone implying he wasn't capable of doing a job he was assigned to.

A flash of skirts caught his eye out the window. He realized the women had come out of the mercantile, their arms piled high with fabrics and other items Lydia planned to use to clean up the school room.

He stood up quickly, grabbing his hat off the hook by his desk and moved outside. Before they could even get across the street to the mercantile, Lewis's stomach tightened as three men approached the women. Lydia and Fiona were laughing and talking to each other, not paying attention to their surroundings as they balanced the items in their arms.

Lydia ran into one of the men who took the opportunity to grab onto her arm, pretending to help her from falling. "A pretty girl like you should really be watching where she's going. There's all kinds of dangerous men around these parts ready to take advantage of a pretty lady."

"Lucky for her, she's got a couple of men who are keeping a close eye on her and won't be letting that happen. But thank you for your concern." Lewis walked right up and made sure the man saw his badge on the front of his vest.

He was almost sure he could hear Brooks

growling behind him and didn't need to be breaking up any fights if he could help it. Reaching out, he took the things out of Lydia's arms, while Brooks reached for his wife's.

"Well, we were just making sure the ladies were safe. Wouldn't have wanted them stepping off the edge of the sidewalk onto the street where they could be trampled by a passing wagon. Or have them run into any of the unsavory people wandering around the town."

Lewis just kept his eyes on the men, nodding to let them know their help was no longer needed.

As they walked past, Brooks turned on Lydia. "This is exactly why you're not staying in town on your own. I won't allow it. I'm still considered your guardian and I say you're coming home with me."

"Brooks, let's walk up to the schoolhouse so we can talk about this without everyone staring at us." People were starting to stop and watch, wondering what the argument on the street was about. Fiona took her husband's arm, smiling up at him and leading him down the street.

The schoolhouse sat on the edge of the town, away from the saloons and other immoral establishments the parents hoped to keep the children away from.

Lewis offered Lydia a smile as they fell in behind Brooks and Fiona. He could see the worry in her eyes about the possibility of Brooks forcing her to live out on the farm with him. Last night, as they'd eaten together, she'd talked about not wanting to be a burden on her brother. She felt so much guilt for everything that had happened over the years and she didn't want him to be responsible for caring for her anymore.

She wanted Brooks to have this time with his new wife and she didn't want to intrude. It was important for her to start making her own life, and that meant living on her own and following the profession she'd been trained for.

Suddenly, he had an idea. "Brooks, I have a suggestion that might just ease your mind a bit."

They'd reached the stairs to the schoolhouse and stopped walking. Brooks turned back to face them, his expression still showing determination. He wasn't backing down on this argument.

"The boardinghouse where I've been living has changed owners and the monthly cost has gone up. I was thinking of looking for a house somewhere in town since I figured I'll likely be staying for a while. How about I get a room in the Merchants Hotel too, so I can be nearby if she needs me? At least until you feel she's safe."

Brooks' jaw moved as he seemed to fight with his frustration and anger. Lewis could understand his worry for his sister. He'd looked after her for a long time and still felt responsible for her.

"And I promise I will personally walk her to the

schoolhouse each day and meet her to bring her back. She will be safer than anyone else in this entire town."

Lewis smiled down at Lydia who was looking up at him with her mouth hanging partway open. "Lewis, you don't have to do that. It's too much. I don't want you to miss out on having your own home because you're having to look after me. I can just go home with Brooks. It would be easier and less worry for everyone."

Lewis's heart lurched at the defeated look on her face. "No. Brooks will either take this offer or none. It's no trouble to me at all and I will enjoy the company each day."

The smile she gave him made his breath catch in his throat.

He hadn't had many opportunities to be a hero in his life but the way she was looking at him now, he was sure she thought he'd just hung the moon.

CHAPTER 3

"I really can't thank you enough. Brooks can be a bit stubborn and difficult to reason with. I know without your offer, I'd have been dragged back out to the farm with him whether I wanted to or not."

She set the chalks and board onto the desk in front of her, then moved on to the next one. School would start tomorrow, so she was spending the day getting her classroom ready. She felt a strange mix of excitement and fear over teaching her first students.

Lewis had walked her over to the school just after lunch and had come back now to escort her back to the hotel. She wasn't thrilled at the prospect of him being assigned to protect her every time she went out but she figured she wouldn't say anything yet. After Brooks had some time to calm down, she could bring it up again and hopefully he'd see she was just fine on her own.

Besides, she wasn't going to complain about having extra time with Lewis each day.

"Well, we had a shootout right on the street in front of the stables today, so I'd say his worry is well-founded."

She whipped her head up to look at him. He was leaning against her desk at the front of the small room. "Was anyone hurt?"

He seemed so calm about the potential danger that took place. He shrugged. "One man was killed, the other is sitting in a cell back at the jailhouse. It was a disagreement over some money owed in a card game."

Lydia cringed. She knew when Brooks had been gambling and sitting at the tables in the saloons, Abilene had started to become more dangerous. He'd had his own run-ins and had taken a bullet more than once. As far as she knew, Lewis had managed to avoid the same fate, unless it'd happened while she'd been gone.

"Aren't you scared, dealing with the lowest of society, who don't care who they kill, every single day?"

She rubbed the chalk between her fingers as she stood facing him across the room. He had his arms crossed over his chest while he leaned on the desk, one booted foot over the other. He looked like he didn't have a care in the world, even after casually mentioning he'd been witness to a gunfight just a few hours ago.

"Most of the riff-raff we deal with around here are just ordinary folks who fell on hard times and don't know how to bring themselves out of it. And the others..." He shrugged again.

She came over and set down the remaining chalks onto her desk.

"Tom's mighty angry, though. Not supposed to be any guns inside town limits, except for the law, so he's intent on making the man in jail be a warning to any others who might try to go against him."

He stood up straight and looked down at her. The bright amber of his eyes made her heart skip a beat. She reached up and nervously patted at her hair, which she knew was likely falling out of the pins she'd put it up in earlier.

He smiled, then looked around the room. "You've made it look nice in here. The kids will be excited to have a teacher who isn't apt to be chased out of town at the first sign of trouble."

"Thanks. I've made up some curtains for the windows so, hopefully, they won't be distracted by all of the excitement happening outside during their lessons."

She picked up her bonnet and placed it on her head, tying the ribbon beneath her chin. Lewis grabbed the shawl she'd thrown over the back of the chair and placed it over her shoulders. As she reached up to take the edges from him, their fingers brushed.

Immediately, a shiver went through her whole body. Her cheeks heated and she hoped he didn't notice the effect he had on her. She treasured his friendship and wouldn't want to scare him away.

She wished she was beautiful and perfect. The kind of woman a man like Lewis wouldn't be able to ignore, no matter what had happened in his past that made him swear he'd never end up tied to a woman.

They walked out the door onto the street and he smiled over, taking her hand, and placing it into the bend of his arm.

"I got my things moved into my room today too. I'm just down the hall from you, so you can sleep safe now, knowing I'm close by."

She laughed silently to herself. Knowing he was nearby wasn't going to make her sleep any easier. She figured it would have just the opposite effect.

"It'll make Brooks feel better, I guess. I feel terrible you've had to do that, just because of his thickheaded insistence. I promise not to become a burden on you."

They walked in silence and as they came by the saloon closest to the school, she felt him pull her in a little closer to his side. She tried to speed up her steps but her leg was aching after standing on it all day and she stumbled a bit.

Lewis reached his other arm around to stop her from falling. "Are you all right?"

Her face burned with embarrassment as she nodded. "I'm fine. I was just trying to walk too fast."

"I'm sorry, I should've been more careful."

Lewis knew her leg was a problem but she didn't know how much he actually knew. Brooks had sheltered her terribly for so many years. When she'd finally started coming around town, she'd had to deal with the stares and whispering she knew happened behind her back.

But she didn't care what most people thought. The only one she wished didn't have to see her imperfection was the man who was looking at her now with concern in his eyes.

She gave him a smile. "It's not your fault. I sometimes forget myself and try doing more than I can."

They stood with the daylight starting to fade over the horizon as she tried to catch her breath. Even though the sun was setting, it hadn't slowed the bustling around town down any. There were still people walking in every direction, horses bounding down the street and from the open door of the saloon, the sound of the piano reached her ears.

The chill of the late fall evening was starting to

come out and he reached up to pull her shawl tighter around her shoulders.

"Does it hurt much?"

He'd never asked her about her injury; in fact, she didn't think anyone had ever asked her. Most people pretended they didn't notice, then waited until she was gone before discussing among themselves what they thought could be the problem.

Somehow, though, she sensed that he truly cared about her answer and wasn't just asking to be curious.

"Just if I stand too long or try walking too fast." She laughed nervously. "Normally, it doesn't really hurt. It's just cumbersome."

He was still holding her shawl as he looked down at her. "What happened? You don't have to tell me if you don't want to but I've always wondered. Brooks never wanted to talk about it and any time I asked, he got angry."

Letting his hands fall, he stuffed them into his pockets. She swallowed against the dryness of her throat as his eyes searched hers.

"I was a bit stubborn when I was a little girl and I kept insisting to my father that I could ride on my own. I loved my horse and desperately wanted to prove I was big enough to do it. Brooks helped me up on the horse one day, even though father had forbidden it unless he was around." She shrugged again as the memories came crashing back.

"The horse got spooked by something and I don't really remember much after that. Except when I woke up, my leg was badly broken. The doctor tried to set it but it didn't heal properly."

She turned and started walking, wanting to keep moving so she didn't have to look into his eyes and see the pity she knew would be there.

"My father tried so hard to find the money to take me to better doctors. One day, when he was in town, he sat at a table with a man who offered him more than he could refuse if he won. He played all of the money he had—money to pay his bills at the seed lot—hoping for the chance to win enough to fix my leg."

She took a deep breath, letting the coolness of the early evening air fill her throat. Lewis put his hand under her elbow to help her as they stepped down to cross the dusty street toward the hotel.

"My father took it hard. Then my ma got sick and died shortly after. He was never the same after that. I'm not even sure what happened but all I know is that Brooks found him one morning in the barn when he went to do chores."

Lewis continued for her, "And that's why Brooks was gambling. I knew he'd mentioned why he was sitting the tables all those years but I never really understood the whole story. He'd confided to me about your father losing the money but he'd left out the part about you being injured."

They were outside the hotel, so she stopped and smiled at him, wanting to lighten the mood from the topic of conversation. "So now, to the townsfolk around here, I'm just that Vaughn girl who walks with a limp. Which is why I'm not even sure what Brooks was so worried about me with staying in town by myself. It's not like I'm the kind of lady who is drawing men's attention everywhere I go."

She gave a laugh to convince him it didn't bother her, even though every word she said tore at her heart. She started to turn and open the door so they could go inside but he held her elbow firm, not letting her move.

She turned back and met amber eyes that didn't show any hint of pity at all.

"Lydia, I think you're fooling yourself if you believe that. In fact, I'd say you're likely just about the most beautiful woman I've ever known. You just need to start believing it yourself."

As she stood with her mouth gaping open, he winked, then opened the door and escorted her inside.

Lewis Kinkaid had just told her she was beautiful. She didn't know if he was being truthful or just feeling sorry for her and wanted to cheer her up.

But, at this point, she didn't care. It was enough to fill her heart for now.

CHAPTER 4

"Good morning, class. My name is Miss Vaughn. I'm so excited to be here and I can't wait to meet all of you. Can you tell me your names?"

Lydia watched the excited faces as each of the children took their turns telling her their names. She got to a small girl at the front with her top two teeth missing and bouncy blonde hair hanging down around her shoulders.

"My name's Mary. My ma told me we wouldn't likely have school this year 'cause no teacher would want to set foot in this wretched abyss full of crooks and good-for-nothing lowlifes."

Lydia almost choked on the laugh that threatened to escape at the honest expression on the little girl's face. For such a small body, she was sure full of colorful words. No doubt she'd been listening to a conversation she wasn't supposed to hear.

"Well, it's nice to meet you, Mary. I grew up around here and I couldn't imagine living anywhere else. It's not so bad." She wanted to move onto the next child before Mary decided to give her some more descriptive words about Abilene.

She walked past Mary and said her greetings to some of the other children. When she got to an older boy near the back, he was leaning far back in his chair with his arms crossed over his chest. He stared straight past her, obviously intent on not acknowledging her.

"And what can I call you?" She smiled at the boy but he still didn't look her way.

Crossing her arms in front of her, she decided now was as good a time as any to show him she wouldn't allow any disrespect in her classroom.

"I'm going to ask you to look at someone when they're speaking to you, and give them an answer when they ask a question."

The boy's head turned but his face didn't have any hint of a smile as he looked at her. "My name's Pete. And beggin' your pardon *ma'am* but I don't want to be here in the first place. So I'd say you're wasting your time if you think I'm going to listen to anything you've got to say."

She tried to keep the shock from her face. She'd been warned there would be students who were more difficult to handle than some of the others but she never thought she'd see it already.

"Well, Pete, I'm going to do my best to change your mind." She knew it best not to engage him in anything right now and to give him some time to warm up to her. Moving to the girl who sat in the seat across from him, she turned and smiled at her. She was an older girl too and her hair was hanging down, covering her face as she looked at the floor.

"And what's your name?" she said the words softly, sensing the girl was shy, and would rather avoid being the center of attention.

"Oh she doesn't talk much. Her name's Elizabeth McCutcheon. Her ma died last year."

"Mary! You mustn't interrupt." The young girl had spoken from her seat at the front of the room. Lydia spun around to put her fingers to her lips to shush Mary, then turned back and smiled at the girl who was finally looking at her. Her eyes were as brown as her hair and her lips were in a firm line, with no hint of a smile.

"Hello, Elizabeth, I'm very glad to meet you." The girl nodded, then looked back down at her hands folded in her lap.

Lydia realized for the first time just how important her job here was going to be. She intended to make a difference in the lives of these children and she was determined she wouldn't be chased away by the lawless town that had scared every other teacher away.

These youngsters needed someone who cared and lucky for them, she had plenty of love to give them.

LEWIS WAITED AT THE DOOR, watching as all the children ran outside after their first day. The happiness on their faces made him smile.

Lydia said good-bye to each of them and when a boy walked up past where she stood near the door, she smiled at him. "Good-bye, Pete. See you tomorrow."

The boy ignored her and kept walking. Lewis saw the flash of pain in her eyes.

"Young man, I believe the lady said something to you." The boy squinted his eyes at him as he met his stare.

"Bye," the word was mumbled through teeth that were clenched together but at least it was something. He pushed past him and out the door.

Shaking his head, Lewis walked into the room.

"Lewis, you really don't need to come and get me every day. You're a sheriff in a town full of criminals itching for a fight, so I'm sure you have better things you could be doing with your time. I won't tell Brooks if you don't." She was busy tidying up her desk.

He smiled to himself. He knew if he didn't do as he'd said, Brooks would have his hide. And besides, he had to admit he looked forward to being able to see her. He wasn't the only lawman in town, so he could afford a few minutes here and there to spend with her.

He put one foot up on a desk and leaned his arms on his leg. "So, how was your first day?"

She flashed the brightest smile he'd ever seen as she began to tell him everything that had happened. His heart skipped a beat at the beauty that shone through on her face as she spoke with such joy. It was obvious how much she loved what she was doing.

After he'd walked her home last night, he'd spent the night tossing and turning, seeing her eyes as she'd talked about her injury. She'd spent so many years hiding at home, afraid of what people would say. Lydia truly didn't think she had anything to offer a man and had decided she was going to dedicate her life to being a schoolteacher instead.

He didn't see why she couldn't have both. He'd always found himself drawn to Lydia, any time she came to town with her brother. He couldn't explain it because she was far from the sort of woman he normally thought he favored. But perhaps that's why he seemed unable to stop thinking about her—because she was different.

He'd spent so many years angry at the woman who'd hurt him, not to mention all the other women who'd proven over the years they couldn't be trusted.

Trust wasn't something he could give easily anymore. As he'd lain in the dark, thinking about the woman down the hall with brown hair and bright blue eyes, he'd realized, out of everyone he knew, she was one of the few people he did trust.

He'd also admitted to himself, his heart had been pulling in her direction for a long time. The worries he'd had about his past had been holding him back. But the smile on her face when she looked at him, and the caring heart he saw in her as they spent more time together, made him realize he'd be a fool to let a woman like her get away from him.

He knew her brother was going to have something to say about it but he could handle Brooks.

What he couldn't handle was the thought of Lydia not returning his feelings. He thought she might feel the same way but she still didn't believe she was worthy of a man's love. In her eyes, even though she'd never come right out and said it, she was damaged.

She had no idea just how wrong she was.

"Did you hear what I said, Lewis? You look like

you're a million miles away." Lydia was smiling at him, standing in front of him with her bonnet already on and her shawl over her shoulders. She had several books in her arms and was carrying the basket she'd used to bring her lunch today.

Quickly, he stood up straight and reached for the books. "Here, let me take those." He wasn't off to a good start at impressing her as she jumped at the loudness of his words. He hadn't meant to shout but she'd caught him off guard. Lewis didn't want her to think he wasn't a gentleman while she tried to hold the heavy books.

"Well, thank you, Lewis, I think." She was looking at him with a strange expression as she handed him the books. It seemed since he'd decided his intentions last night, he was acting like a young schoolboy with a crush on the teacher.

Clearing his throat, he moved to the door. "We better get going. I'd like to have you back at the hotel before the riff-raff take over the streets."

She rolled her eyes at him. "You sound like Brooks. I don't need two of you hovering over me."

They walked along in silence, saying hello to people they knew and those who stopped to ask how her first day at school went. When they got in front of the mercantile, she stopped and turned. "I need to pick up a few things for class tomorrow. Do you mind?"

He knew Tom would be waiting for him so they

could do their rounds of the saloons but how could he say no?

Going inside, he stood back while she looked for the items she needed. He heard her give a small gasp as she looked behind one counter. "What's wrong?" He walked over to see what had caught her attention.

"Isn't it lovely?"

He squinted as he looked behind the glass. It was a hair comb with some kind of jewels and beads on it. "I guess so. I'm not sure it would look good in my hair, though."

She looked over at him with an eyebrow in the air. "No, I'm sure it wouldn't." They laughed as she went to pay for her items, then walked outside.

"Something like that wouldn't be very practical for a woman like me anyway. When would I wear something so nice? It's not like I have men knocking my door down to court me." The small laugh she gave didn't fool him. He could feel the hurt she held in her heart, believing she wouldn't find a man who could see what she had to offer.

He knew then that he didn't care what it took. He was going to be the man who showed her.

CHAPTER 5

Standing at the window, she watched the children running around past the tree outside. Some of the younger ones were playing tag, while a couple of the older boys threw the ball or tried to hit it with the bat. It was a cool day and the feel of approaching winter was starting to fill the air but the warmth from the woodstove kept the small schoolroom feeling cozy and comfortable.

She couldn't believe she'd been teaching here over two weeks already. She loved the children and looked forward to every day she was here with them. On the weekends, she'd work on her lesson plans and on Sundays, she went to church with Brooks and Fiona. Lewis would always tag along with them and they often spent the afternoon walking or having a picnic lunch outside of town.

Lewis was still insistent on walking her to and from school each day. They'd usually eat their evening meals together in the hotel restaurant—if he wasn't busy making an arrest or dealing with some other situation. She was enjoying the company, even if she knew it would never be more than friendship.

Brooks had told her once that many women had tried to catch Lewis's eye over the years but he wasn't interested in settling down any time soon. That didn't stop her heart from skipping a beat every time he came near her, though.

Shaking her head to clear the thoughts that always seemed to wander to Lewis, she moved from the window. Turning, she smiled at Elizabeth who was wringing the cloth in the small bucket of water she'd prepared for her to use. "You've done a good job. Thank you for helping me, Elizabeth."

She'd asked her to stay in and help clean the classroom, and she could hear the girl wiping the desks behind her. Elizabeth still didn't speak much and then only when called on. She struggled with her reading which embarrassed the girl knowing there were younger children who were already reading better than her.

Lydia wanted to try talking to her without the others present to see if she could figure out a way to help her.

"Can I go outside now?" Lydia knew even if the young girl did go out, she'd walk to the far corner of the school grounds and sit under the tree by herself like she always did.

"Why don't we sit down and visit for a while? I've never had much chance to talk to you."

The girl just stared at her with her eyes so wide they almost filled her entire face.

She went and sat at her desk, pulling a chair up and patting the seat beside her. Elizabeth came over and sat down but wouldn't bring her eyes to look at her.

"Why don't you tell me a little bit about yourself, Elizabeth? I'd love to hear about you." How could she get the girl to open up to her?

All she did was shrug. "I dunno. I don't really have anything to tell."

"Oh, but you must. How old are you?"

"Eleven."

"That's a wonderful age. Do you have any brothers or sisters?" Lydia knew she didn't have any in school but wondered if there were more at home perhaps.

"No."

This wasn't going as well as she'd planned.

"Do you enjoy school, Elizabeth? Is there anything you'd like to learn about, that I could perhaps be teaching the class?" Maybe if she gave the girl a chance to have a say in what they were learning, she might be more open.

"No. Except I'd like to not have to do the reading. I don't like it when I can't read like the other kids."

Lydia's breath caught as Elizabeth finally lifted her head and looked at her. The poor girl. She knew it was hard for her and now that she'd opened up a bit, perhaps she'd be willing to let her help.

"Why don't we try doing a little reading, right now, without any of the other children around? Would you be willing to do that with me?"

Elizabeth shrugged and looked back down at her hands lying on her skirt.

Grabbing a book before the girl changed her mind, she opened it and pointed to a place for her to start reading. Elizabeth took the book from her and held it with trembling hands.

As Lydia listened to her stumbling over the words, her heart ached. It didn't seem fair that Elizabeth had never been able to learn how to read. Perhaps she'd just never had the right teacher.

"That was good, Elizabeth. How about we spend our lunch times together, cleaning the classroom and working on your reading? Would that be all right?"

Elizabeth's eyes shone with unshed tears and Lydia didn't know if it was from the frustration of trying to read or happiness that maybe someone could teach her. But the girl nodded and gave her the first small smile she'd ever seen on her face.

Suddenly, voices were shouting outside and she raced over to open the door wide. Pete was on top of one of the other boys. They were yelling at each other as they rolled around on the ground, Pete ending up on top.

"You cheated!"

"No I didn't. Get off me!"

Lydia went down the steps as fast as her leg would allow and grabbed Pete by the collar. The boy was too big for her and she couldn't move him. He swung to hit the smaller boy beneath him but his fist hit her in the jaw. Everything felt like it had slowed down as her leg buckled beneath her and she crumpled to the ground.

Mary ran over and fell down beside her. "Miss Vaughn. Are you all right? Please, tell me you aren't dead!"

If not for the pain in her jaw and leg at the moment, Lydia would have laughed out loud at the seriousness of Mary's words. She was always a bit melodramatic.

She sat up, smiling at the small girl beside her as she rubbed at her jaw. The boys had stopped fighting and were standing, looking at the ground in front of them. Elizabeth had followed her outside and now she reached down for Lydia's hand to help her up. As she met her worried gaze, she gave the girl a gentle smile too, letting her know she was okay.

She stood, brushing off her skirts. Suddenly, Lewis rode in on his horse and leaped down before it had even stopped moving. "What's going on here?" He raced over to her and took her shoulders to make her face him. "Are you hurt?"

"I'm fine, Lewis. I just fell, that's all."

"Really? You expect me to believe you just fell? Those boys were fighting as I was getting on my horse to head out of town. I was about to come over here to break it up when I saw you go racing in like a stampeding bull. Next thing I know, I look and you're on the ground."

Lewis's face was red with anger as he spun to face the boys but he kept one hand on her shoulder. "Does anyone want to tell me what happened here?"

"Lewis, really, it's fine."

He looked back at her and shook his head. "No, it isn't fine." He leaned in closer to her and turned her to face him completely again. Reaching up, he gently touched her jaw. "You're getting a bruise." As he looked at her face, the muscles in his jaw worked as he fought to control his anger.

"Please, don't scare them. They know they did wrong." She kept her voice quiet as she pleaded with her eyes.

He swallowed hard, then turned back to face the

children standing around. He walked closer to the boys who stood rooted to the spot, afraid to look at him.

"Boys, you're lucky Miss Vaughn is so kind. If I had my way, I'd be dragging you home by the ears to let your parents know what you did. I won't do anything this time but I'm warning you, if I have to come back here again because of you fighting, you won't be getting off so easy. Understand?" He waited until they both nodded their heads.

He walked to his horse and threw his leg up over the saddle. Grabbing the reins, he looked over to Lydia. "I'll be back to get you after school." With that, he spun his horse around and raced out of town to wherever he was headed previously.

None of the children said anything and she suddenly realized she was shaking. It was chilly outside, so she clapped her hands together and told them to get back inside for their afternoon lessons.

Pete and the other boy stood perfectly still in the same spots they'd been in when Lewis left. "We're mighty sorry, ma'am. It won't happen again."

She was surprised Pete would even take the time to apologize. She nodded her head but needed them to know that what they did wasn't acceptable. "You will both be cleaning the floors for me after school for the next two weeks. And if that behavior ever happens again, I will let Mr. Kinkaid take care of you."

Walking into the classroom, she held her chin high as she made her way back up to her desk. Even though she was putting on a brave face, the truth was, she'd been reminded once again of her weakness. Her leg hadn't been able to hold her up and she'd fallen in front of everyone.

She was humiliated that Lewis had seen it too.

The room was quiet as the children probably all wondered what she would do. "Are you going to quit and leave us too?" Mary's sad voice reached her ears.

She turned to look at the classroom. "No, Mary, of course not. I told you, this is my home. I'm not going anywhere. Besides, I've got a lot of reasons right here to stay." She smiled around at the faces before her, all with cheeks red from the chill outside.

"And it's not like Mr. Kinkaid would let you go anyway." The children all laughed nervously as Mary spoke out loud again.

"I don't know what you mean, Mary." She turned to her desk to get her lesson book, hoping no one had noticed the burning that had reached her cheeks.

"Of course you do, Miss Vaughn. Mr. Kinkaid is smitten with you. It's as obvious as the eyes on my face."

She dropped the book onto her desk at the child's attempt at grown-up words again. Turning to face Mary to scold her once more for saying personal things without thinking, she felt her mouth drop as all the other children nodded, agreeing with Mary.

Well, they were all just children. What could they possibly know about love?

CHAPTER 6

"So, I heard a rumor around town that you're paying an awful lot of attention to the new schoolteacher who also happens to be Brooks Vaughn's sister."

Lewis rolled his eyes at the man across the table from him. They sat in the tavern having lunch and his friend hadn't wasted any time getting under his skin.

"Not sure what you heard but I do know it's none of your business." He wasn't in the mood to be discussing Lydia with anyone, even if it was an old friend.

He'd been friends with Harrison Winchester since they were young boys and had attended boarding school with him. He was part of the Winchester fortune and both he and Lewis had decided they had better things to do than attend school. They'd been unruly and rowdy, eventually getting kicked out. No one would ever suspect that the man who now enforced the law was once one of those boys who didn't believe in following any rules.

The men had eventually parted ways. Lewis came west, becoming a sheriff and settling in Abilene. Harrison had come along just over a year ago after drifting around for a while trying to find himself. Now, not only had he found himself, he'd inherited his own ranch and was happily married, living in a small town not too far from Abilene.

Harrison's laughter grated on his nerves. "Well, from what I've been told, you've been walking her to the schoolhouse and back every day. You've been dining together. You do know, a schoolteacher has a certain reputation to uphold. I'm sure you can't be surprised the townsfolk are concerned about the local sheriff possibly stealing their schoolteacher."

He kept his eyes on Harrison's, determined to let him see he wasn't enjoying the topic of conversation. "I appreciate your concern for Lydia's reputation but, I assure you, as far as the townsfolk opinions are concerned, I don't give a fig. They know Lydia's just about the only woman prepared to teach in this town, so I'm sure the rules governing her reputation won't be put into question."

"So you admit you're paying the lovely lady some attention?" Harrison chuckled to himself as he took a spoonful of the soup and put it to his mouth.

Lewis looked out the window and down the street toward the far end of town where the school was. "Yes, I'll admit it. But, I don't know what good it'll do me anyway."

"You mean there's a woman who isn't throwing herself at your feet?"

He turned back and shook his head. "Far from it. In fact, I'm sure she has no idea I'm even interested in her. She seems to think she doesn't have anything that would attract a man. I just can't figure her out."

"It's been my experience that most women are like that." Harrison was nodding his head to himself as he continued eating.

"I've offered to take her out to Brooks and Fiona's after church on Sunday, so I'm hoping the ride out will give us a chance to talk. In town, it seems like there's always someone watching. I don't even know what I'm planning on saying. It's not like I've had a lot of luck when it comes to the opposite sex. And I don't need to be setting myself up to have my heart stomped on again."

Harrison was smiling as he pushed his bowl away. "I'd be more worried about Brooks stomping on you if you do anything to compromise his sister."

"I can handle Brooks. It's his sister I'm having trouble with."

"THANKS FOR TAKING me out to the farm for the day. It was nice to be home and to have a real home cooked meal. Not that I don't love Mrs. Malloy's cooking, it's just nice to have something made at home."

She knew she was rambling on, trying to make conversation as they made their way back to town. After she'd mentioned to him yesterday that she hadn't ridden a horse since her accident, Lewis had arranged for a wagon to use for the day.

Now they rode back to town with the setting sun bringing a cool chill into the air. She pulled her shawl tight and rubbed her arms for warmth. Lewis reached into the back of the wagon and pulled something out. "Here, I thought it might get cool on the ride home so I threw in an extra blanket." He took the reins into one hand, opened the blanket and tucked it around her shoulders with the other.

The moon made its way into the sky, illuminating the ground ahead of them for miles. She turned her head slightly to catch a glimpse of Lewis's face, smiling to herself at his thoughtfulness.

"How are the reading lessons going with Elizabeth? Has she improved at all?"

"Oh, I can't believe I forgot to tell you! I noticed she was squinting a great deal when she tried to read. I took her to Dr. Hastings who did some tests for her eyes. It turns out she needs glasses. He's sure once she can see properly, she'll be able to learn to read. Poor girl didn't realize there was anything wrong with how she was seeing things."

Lewis turned and smiled at her, shaking his head. "You really are a special woman, Lydia Vaughn. Most people would've just given up on that girl and not done anything to help her."

Her entire body warmed at his compliment. "I'm not really special, Lewis. I was just doing what a teacher should do."

He stared at her for a moment, then pulled on the reins, instructing the horses to stop. Her heart leaped into her throat. *What was he doing?*

He turned to face her, reaching out and pulling the edges of the blanket closer around her neck. "Lydia, remember that day when those boys were fighting and you got thrown to the ground?"

She nodded, unsure what he was getting at.

He kept his eyes on hers, the amber color reflecting in the brightness of the moon. "I wanted to take those boys and give them a thrashing. When I saw you fall, I truly felt like my heart had been wrenched from my chest. But when I got there, you didn't want to scare them. You could have let me haul them off and try to scare them straight but you were more worried about them than yourself."

She was still reeling from what he'd said about his heart being wrenched from his chest. *What did he mean by that?* He sat staring at her for the longest time and she felt like her own heart was doing a dance. He lifted his hand to touch her face. Realizing he still wore his glove, he yanked it from his hand, then let his skin touch hers.

"Surely you know how much you mean to me, Lydia."

She still hadn't said anything and as his fingers moved to her neck, he pulled the pieces of hair out that were tucked into the blanket. Her skin tingled with every motion he made. Opening her mouth to try and speak, she found her throat was too dry to even make a sound.

Lewis was looking at her lips and she swallowed hard, desperately trying to get rid of the dryness. His head came toward her and his lips caught hers with the gentlest of kisses. He lifted his head up and smiled down into her eyes.

"I've been wanting to do that for a very long time, Lydia Vaughn."

Her lips burned where he'd touched them and her body was screaming for him not to pull away yet.

But he sat back up and grinned at her. "I've never heard you speechless before."

She realized she was still sitting in the exact same position she'd been in when he first stopped the wagon. She hadn't spoken a word and she hadn't even moved her hands from where they held the blanket. Instead, she sat with her mouth still gaping open, staring at the man who'd just flipped her stomach upside down.

Snapping her mouth closed, she turned and faced forward as he flicked the reins to get the wagon moving. When she finally got the courage to peek back over at him, she was sure her cheeks caught fire when she saw him looking at her.

The smile he gave her took her breath away. Could it be possible that the man she'd been in love with for so long might return those feelings for her? She'd never thought it would be possible but after tonight, she realized nothing this man did should surprise her.

CHAPTER 7

"I promise, I won't let you fall."

She tugged the collar of her jacket up tighter, blocking out the coolness of the day as the sky threatened to give them an early snow. "Couldn't we wait until it's warmer outside? Like maybe summer?"

She really didn't feel ready to hop up onto the back of the mare Lewis was holding in front of her. It was his own horse and one he said he trusted with his life. "Lydia, you can't spend the rest of your life afraid to get back on a horse. And waiting until it's warmer won't make any difference. Besides, the day's cool enough that I won't be as likely to get dragged away by a couple of drunks fighting in the street. It's too cold for most of them to even come outside today."

The sky was gray and dreary, with no hint of the

sun anywhere. Mrs. Malloy said she could feel the snow coming in her bones. When Lewis had knocked on her door this morning and asked if she'd like to take a walk, she'd been thrilled. Since the other night in the wagon, they'd seemed to move to a comfortable place between them as they got to know each other better.

She didn't think she'd ever been so happy in her life. Well, that was until they'd gotten out on the street and he'd said he was taking her to the stables. There was a small pen out back and he'd arranged for her to try some riding.

She patted the horse's nose and whispered softly to it, "Please, just walk slowly and don't throw me off. The sooner we get this over with, the sooner we can both get back inside where it's warm."

Lewis walked right up beside her and leaned in where she was up against the mare's nose. "Ruby's a smart horse but even she can't understand what you're saying."

He kept his voice to a whisper too.

Stepping back, she lifted her chin and rolled her eyes. "Well, you don't know that for sure."

"Come on, I promise I won't let go of the reins." He gave her a smile that would melt butter and put his hand out to her.

She held his gaze for a moment, then finally put her hand in his. "Fine, but I'm holding you responsible if I fall."

"I promise. If you fall, I'll catch you."

The way he said the words, with such promise and feeling, she was sure her legs were going to give out beneath her. How could he make one sentence cause her entire heart to feel like it was about to land on the ground at her feet?

He held her hand while she put her good leg in the stirrup. As soon as she had her foot steady, he reached behind and put his hands on her waist. Looking in her eyes, he smiled down. "Are you ready?"

All she could do was nod and he was lifting her. She threw her other leg over the top the best she could but she struggled to lift it above the back of the saddle. The split skirt she'd worn this morning was bulky, catching on the clasp of the saddle. But Lewis was there and he held her firmly while he helped her lift her other leg the rest of the way over.

She would've far rather stayed in his arms than be thrown up onto the back of a horse that could decide to throw her at any moment.

However, Lewis wanted to help her get over her fear and she knew he wasn't the type to just let this go until she at least tried.

The first thing she did was grab the front of the saddle with both hands and clenched her legs tightly so she wouldn't fall. "Loosen up your legs or you'll confuse Ruby. Just try to relax. I'll hand you the reins but don't worry, I won't let go of the lead rope.

I know you remember how to do this, you just need to be reminded."

She tried to ignore the fact that she was sitting on top of an animal that had the power to run with her on it at any given time. She pretended she couldn't hear her heart beating so loudly it was hurting her ears.

"Lydia, you have to relax. Try to remember how you used to feel when you were on your horses. I know you told me one time how much you used to love them. And how you loved riding when your father would lead you. You've waited a long time to ride on your own." He was smiling at her but she wasn't comfortable enough yet to smile back. In fact, she was afraid to move any part of her body and that included her lips.

Lewis tugged on the rope and Ruby started to walk. Lydia clung for dear life onto the reins, trying to remember how to tell the horse what she wanted it to do. All she could remember was the fear she'd felt the last time she'd been in a saddle and the horse was running at breakneck speed out of the pen.

The motion of the horse moving stopped and Lewis was over beside her looking up. He reached up to take the reins in his hand too. Before she knew what he was doing, he'd swung his leg up and was sitting right behind her.

Every part of her body was touching his front,

and his arms came around her to help hold the reins. Where a moment ago she'd been terrified and cold, she was now enjoying the security of his arms and the warmth from his body next to hers.

He bent his head down and spoke in her ear, "Just trust me, okay? As long as I'm here, I'm not going to let anything happen."

He started walking the mare and, within just a few seconds, she started to feel the familiar tug at her heart she'd always felt as a little girl riding on the back of her horse. She felt free and alive and she soon realized she'd completely relaxed in Lewis's arms.

She decided she'd be happy even if the horse did decide to throw her if it meant she'd spend her last moments on Earth in this man's arms.

They rode around in silence for what seemed like forever as she learned the rhythm and feel of the horse beneath her again. Her cheeks were cold but she, suddenly, didn't care about the cold anymore.

"Do you think you'd like to try it on your own?" His voice startled her as she realized she'd let herself lean completely back onto his chest. But he hadn't said anything, so she hadn't even noticed.

She instantly sat back up and held her grip more firmly on the reins. "I think so. But don't let go of the rope."

Her entire body screamed in protest when he hopped back to the ground. The cold seeped through her clothes when the heat he'd provided went missing. He grabbed the rope at the front and smiled up at her as she gained her confidence back. Every step the horse took helped her heart to finally slow down.

"You can let go now." He stood in the middle of the pen, holding the rope as Ruby slowly walked around, her breath showing in the air as she snorted. No one else was back here with them, all the animals were inside the stables with the cold that was settling in.

As she said the words, he smiled up at her. "Are you sure?"

She nodded and felt her pulse quicken as he let go of the rope. The one and only other time she'd ridden on her own hadn't ended well. But it was what she'd always dreamed of doing.

Ruby trotted around Lewis, seeming to sense her fear and wanting to prove she could be trusted. Her mane blew in the wind as she followed the commands Lydia sent to her.

Finally, Lewis caught the rope as she went by, stopping Ruby with a light rub on the nose as he looked up at Lydia. She knew her smile had to be covering her face because no matter how hard she tried, she couldn't bring it under control. "Did you see that? I rode by myself."

Lewis was grinning up at her. "I knew you could."

She met his eyes. "Thank you."

He put his hand up for her to take. She swung her leg back over the way she'd come up and, as she got it over the top, he grabbed her waist again. Pulling her gently back, she fell into his arms and he turned her to face him.

Her hands went up to his shoulders as she tried to steady her legs. The wind picked up around them and she was sure she'd never felt as warm as she did at this moment, looking up into his eyes.

"You're welcome." His smile was her undoing and she found herself moving onto her toes and putting her hand up to pull his head forward. She knew she was acting wanton but she didn't care. She'd worry about that later.

Right now, all she knew was that being in his arms felt right.

He met her lips and she could feel the blood pulsing through her veins. She found her fingers tightening around the collar of his jacket, holding him close. His arms went around her waist as his lips moved on hers and she was sure the world around them had stopped moving.

Suddenly, the sound of a bugle from an approaching stagecoach tore through the air. He pulled his head back but didn't let her go. His eyes met hers and she noticed the small lines around his eyes from smiling. "If I'd have known how you'd pay me for your riding lessons, I reckon I'd have been throwing you up on that saddle long ago."

She realized how improper she'd acted and tried to pull away. "I should get back to my room. I have to get the lessons ready for the week." Even with the coldness in the air biting at her skin, she could feel the heat rise in them as he still held her firmly in his arms.

"I'll take you home, on the condition you share your meal with me later."

Afraid someone would walk back and catch them like this, she quickly agreed, hoping he'd let her go.

Chuckling to himself, he grabbed Ruby's lead rope and they walked into the stable to put her away. The stable boy came over and took the reins, knowing Sheriff Kinkaid liked to keep his horse at the ready in case she was needed. He said he'd rub Ruby down and give her some feed like he always did.

Lewis escorted her out to the front and they watched as the stagecoach bounced into town, then turned to make their way back to the hotel. Lydia was sure her life couldn't be happier than it was right now. Abilene might not be the most beautiful town in the West but here she had a teaching job she loved and a man who'd worked his way into her heart.

It was all she'd ever needed.

"Lewis! Lewis Kinkaid!" A woman's voice reached her ears from behind them, so she stopped and turned.

"Lewis, there's a woman calling you." Lewis had stopped but he was staring straight ahead. As she looked at him, she was sure his color had gone whiter than the snow that was threatening to fall.

Slowly he turned and the woman ran and threw herself into his arms. Lydia stood in shock, taking note of the rich velvet material of the woman's coat. She found herself looking down at her own old coat made of sturdier fabric for life out here.

The woman's hair was fiery red and the satin gloves she wore were now clasping Lewis's cheeks as she stepped back to look up into his face.

"Oh, my darling. I've missed you so much."

Lydia's heart clenched and she was sure she'd stopped breathing. Lewis turned his head and met her eyes as he took the woman's arms and held her away from him.

"Lydia..."

"Lewis, who's this?" Lydia interrupted him, her voice shaking as she kept her gaze on his.

"I'm sorry. I didn't even see you there. My name is Rose Parker, Lewis's fiancée."

CHAPTER 8

"Darling, is this really the best hotel in town? Are you nearby? I have concerns about my safety and I'm not sure I'll be able to sleep a wink."

"Rose, Abilene doesn't have much else to offer, so this is the best you'll find." He threw her bags onto her bed, then turned back to face her. "And, I'd appreciate if you don't call me darling. You know as well as I do that's not true. Not anymore."

He didn't bother to tell her that the hotel he'd brought her to was on the opposite side of the street to where he was staying. And that he knew there'd been rooms available in his hotel. This one was closer to the school but he hoped he'd be able to rid himself of Rose soon enough that he wouldn't have to worry about the possibility of her causing any trouble.

"Are you still sore that I put off our wedding?"

She gave him the smile that had always left his stomach turned inside out. He noticed now how little effect it had on him now.

Raising an eyebrow, he leaned against the doorframe. “Is that what you call running off a week before we were to be wed, to go on an ‘adventure’ to New York?”

“Lewis, you knew I was going to stay with my cousin. She’d written to me, talking about the fun she was having and asked me to join her before I got married. She was having the time of her life, attending balls with the Astors and so many of the elite. It was a once in a lifetime opportunity for me. You always knew I was coming back.”

He couldn’t believe what he was hearing. She truly believed what she’d done was no big deal. He’d been young, naïve, and so sure she was in love with him. That was until something more exciting came along and off she went, telling him to wait for her.

He’d packed up his things shortly after that and left New Haven. His father hadn’t made life easy, insisting he go after her and bring her back so they could go through with the marriage that would be beneficial to their families.

She might think they were still engaged to be married but as far as he was concerned, that had ended the day she told him she was leaving.

“So you think you can just waltz back in here

and find me and everything will go back to the way it was? In case you hadn't noticed, I've moved on."

"Well, yes. I went and talked to your father when I got back. He told me where I could find you. He says he's hopeful you've come to your senses and will now be willing to go through with the marriage. I'm supposed to tell you he's prepared to make it worth your while to come back home and resume your life there." She was smiling at him widely, knowing full well that meant he'd become a wealthy man if he went back to New Haven.

He laughed loudly. "In other words, you didn't get any better offers with your society men in New York. And you thought I'd still just be waiting for you and at least you'd still get your hands on my family's money."

The room went quiet as she stood frozen to the spot. "Is that what you think?"

"That's exactly what I think. Can you deny that my family's wealth wasn't part of your attraction to me? What if I told you that I don't want anything to do with the money and I have no intentions of ever leaving my life here. Would you still be interested?"

"Well...well...your father said you'd walked away from the money but he figured you'd come back once you saw me." Her voice didn't sound so sure anymore.

"My father was wrong. I'm not leaving. But you are."

She ran over and placed her hand on his arm. "Please, darling. You can't just send me away without seeing if the feelings we had aren't still there."

He stood up straight, pulling his arm from her grip. "Rose, you're free to do whatever you want. You can stay or you can leave—it makes no difference to me. But I have someone who means a great deal to me, who I have to go and try explaining all of this to." He tipped his head to the side and squinted his eyes tight.

"But of course you knew that, didn't you? You saw me with her when you stepped off that stagecoach and you couldn't wait to throw yourself into my arms to lay your claim."

"That mouse of a girl you were walking with? I didn't think any such thing. She's not exactly the kind of woman you'd be attracted to."

As he looked at this woman, who he'd once thought he loved and couldn't live without, he realized just how lucky he'd been to avoid a life tied to her. He should be thanking her for leaving all those years ago.

Thanks to her, he'd followed his own dreams. He'd come out west to work as a lawman and found a woman he knew he *could* spend his life with. However, he was sure that woman hated him right now more than anything and he didn't know what to do to change her mind.

All he knew was he wasn't going to stop until he did.

❧

THE SOUND of yelling outside the window had all the children jumping from their seats to see what was going on.

"Children, get back in your seats." She clapped her hands and went over to shoo them back from where they were peeking out the glass at the commotion outside.

"It looks like Sheriff Kinkaid's horse, ma'am."

She looked over Pete's head to see what Lewis was doing. As she watched, she realized he was hunched over and holding his side. The sound of her scream reached her ears before she even realized it was her. Lewis fell from his horse, landing on the ground in a heap while the people who'd been on the street ran toward him.

Without thinking, she turned to go outside, holding the railing on the stairs as she tried to make her legs move faster. She had to get to him. She could see him up the street and it seemed like he was so far away. No matter how fast she tried to go, it didn't seem like she was getting any closer.

"Someone get Dr. Hastings! He's been shot!" The words rang in her ears louder than the train whistle as it came through town.

She was almost to him when a blur of red velvet came from nowhere and threw herself on the ground beside him. "No! Lewis, darling, please don't die on me!"

The pain in her heart at seeing the other woman with him stopped her in her tracks and she was unable to move another step. "We have to get him to the doctor's office."

A few of the men who'd gathered around worked together by picking him up and carrying him the rest of the way to Dr. Hastings office. The woman in red velvet followed behind, her wails cutting through the silence in the street.

Unable to stand any longer, Lydia's legs collapsed beneath her, and she slid to the ground in the middle of the street. She'd desperately needed to see him, to know he was all right, but it wasn't her place.

She just sat, watching as they went into the doctor's, leaving her sitting on the street with her skirts around her.

"Ma'am?" Pete's voice quietly spoke from behind her and he gently placed her shawl over her shoulders. She hadn't even realized how cold the wind was that blew around her.

The boy reached down and offered his hand to help her up. She looked behind him and saw all her students huddled around. The older children had their hands on the shoulders of the younger ones and they all looked at her with worry on their young faces.

She let Pete help her up, then put her arms around Mary and another girl, leading them back to the classroom.

"I think, today, we'll end our classes early. I'm sure Sheriff Kinkaid will be fine but I'll go and check on him so I can let you all know for sure tomorrow."

Her voice shook as she tried to get her feelings under control. She knew she would need to calm the children down before sending them home.

As the world seemed to be spinning out of control around her, she desperately fought to keep herself from falling apart in front of the children any more than they'd already witnessed.

She needed to see Lewis. And she didn't care what the woman in red had to say about it.

CHAPTER 9

She opened the door to the building, her heart in her throat. She'd already heard the talk around town saying how Lewis had been shot going with Tom Smith to serve a warrant on a farmer outside of town who was wanted for murder. Apparently, they'd been ambushed. Lewis had been able to report what had happened before he lost consciousness, so the other men working for Tom had raced out to find the men responsible.

Sadly, Tom had been killed and Lewis would've been too if he hadn't managed to get away and back to town for help.

The whole town was in shock and gripped in fear, wondering at the lawlessness that would come back now that the firm-handed marshal was dead. Lewis would have to be in charge until they could get another man sent out but he was lying on a table in the doctor's office with a bullet in his side.

And she didn't even know how bad he was. No one seemed to know except the doctor and the woman everyone was whispering about—Rose, his fiancée.

When her eyes adjusted to the dimness of the room, she realized the woman in question was sitting in a chair right in front of her. It was too late to turn and leave, so she lifted her chin and walked inside.

She needed to know how Lewis was and she was willing to swallow her pride long enough to find out.

The red-haired beauty sat watching her with tear-stained eyes. "What are you doing here?"

Lydia clenched her jaw against the retort that was on the tip of her tongue. "How's Lewis doing?"

Rose shrugged. "I'm waiting to hear more from the doctor."

Lydia sat on the edge of the other seat across the room. "My name is Lydia Vaughn."

Rose smirked at her. "Yes, I know who you are. You're the schoolteacher here, aren't you?"

She wasn't sure why but the way Rose said the word *schoolteacher*, it felt like she was trying to insult her. Putting on the sincerest smile she could muster, she replied, "I am. A rewarding job that will help shape the future of the children of this town."

Rose chuckled softly to herself. "Yes, I suppose it

is. Teaching is a very noble profession for spinsters. I've known a few women who didn't have any prospects for marriage who've had wonderful careers as teachers."

Thankfully, the doctor came out from the other room. He looked between the two women, obviously uncomfortable. It was no secret around town that Lydia had been spending time with Lewis until Rose had shown up. "Um, Miss Vaughn. Lewis has asked me to find you but since you're already here, he'd like to talk to you."

The fury in Rose's eyes was felt across the room but she decided to ignore it. She needed to see Lewis for herself, so she didn't care what the other woman thought. It was obvious, though, that Dr. Hastings was having some serious concerns for his own safety after having to pass on the message in front of the other woman.

She stood, walking with as much strength as she could to keep herself from limping openly. Even though she tried to pretend it didn't bother her, she was still self-conscious about her uneven gait and it seemed even more pronounced now with the stunning redheaded woman watching her.

The doctor held the door open for her, then closed it softly behind her as she went in. She walked slowly toward the small cot that was set up in the corner of the room where Lewis lay with his arm up covering his eyes.

At the sound of someone coming into the room, he brought his arm down slowly, then tried to sit up when he realized who it was. "Lydia."

His voice sounded strained and he grimaced with pain when he moved. "Lewis, just stay lying down." She put her hand out to press onto his shoulder, pleading with him to not do anything that would cause him more pain.

He reached up and grabbed her hand in his before she could move it away.

"Lydia, please give me a chance to explain. You've been avoiding me for days."

She'd asked Mr. Malloy to walk her to the school each day since Rose had shown up and she suspected Edna had spoken with Lewis, asking him to give her some space.

"I don't want to talk about that right now. I just wanted to check and make sure you're all right. No matter what else has happened, I don't wish you to be hurt."

His hand had surprising strength for a man who'd just been shot. He pulled her close, wincing slightly. "Rose is not my fiancée. Not anymore."

She swallowed hard, trying to keep the tears that were threatening from spilling over.

"Lewis, she's beautiful and she obviously loves you. Whatever happened between the two of you isn't my concern. I just wanted to make sure you were going to be all right. Brooks would want to know."

She pulled her hand from his and turned to go, avoiding his eyes. She knew too well how easily his gaze could cause her senses to fall apart. "I'll send Rose in now. She's been worried."

"Lydia, please."

His voice sounded pained but she figured it was from the bullet wound he'd just had stitched up. She went into the other room and nodded to the other two before taking her leave.

The minute she walked out the door, she let the tears flow as she leaned back against the wall. She let the anguish of the last few days come out, no longer caring who saw her.

She was grieving the loss of someone she loved as surely as she would if he'd been killed by that bullet.

"You better have a good explanation for what's going on here or you might find yourself wishing that bullet had finished you." Brooks was sitting in the only other chair in his room, leaning back with his arms crossed in front of him. Lewis was in the softer chair, with his legs up on the edge of the bed, holding the bandage that was wrapped around his waist.

The bullet had gone right through his side and had, thankfully, missed hitting anything vital. He knew it could've been much worse and as he remembered the scene with Tom Smith, he closed his eyes and cringed. It was something he'd never be able to forget and it haunted him every time he tried to sleep.

And as if that wasn't enough, he was dealing with a woman who couldn't seem to understand how serious he was about wanting her to leave. And now an angry brother to the only woman he did want near him.

He opened his eyes and turned to look out the window beside him. He'd been stuck in his room for a couple of days now, on the doctor's orders, and he was ready to get back outside. The snow that had been threatening the other day never happened and now it looked like the weather had decided to give them a few more days of warmth before the winter.

His heart lurched as he noticed Lydia walking beside Fiona into the mercantile. "How's she doing?" His voice sounded strained to his ears.

"Lydia's tough. She's been through worse." Brooks wasn't giving him much else.

He turned his head to face Brooks. He knew his friend wanted answers. He'd always been protective of his sister and when it had started to appear that something was happening between them, Brooks had watched things closely.

Brooks wasn't happy to find out the man he'd called a friend, who he'd trusted not to hurt his sister, had been engaged to another woman.

"Brooks, I've told Lydia and I'm telling you the same. I'm not engaged to Rose. We were engaged a long time ago but it never happened. She has it in her head that just because things didn't work out for her in New York, she can just come back in like nothing happened."

"Did you love her?"

Brooks wasn't going to let this go easily.

"I thought I did. But we were young. And I was a hotheaded young man who actually believed a woman might be able to fall in love with me and not my family's money."

"So why haven't you told Lydia you were engaged? Or that your family has money for that matter? Surely you don't think she's the kind of woman who would base her love for you on how much money you have."

"No, I haven't told her any of this. It just never came up. Lydia is still so insecure, sometimes. She's the toughest girl I know with most things. But when it comes to her—and her worth—she just seems to be afraid to believe she has anything to offer. I didn't want to scare her off."

Brooks just shrugged. "Well, I don't envy your position, that's for sure."

Lewis scowled at him. "What's that supposed to mean?"

Brooks stood up and came over to slap him on the shoulder. He walked to the door, then turned back to face him. "Just that I know my sister. She might be insecure about certain things but she's also just about the most stubborn person I've ever known. And it's going to take more than that smile of yours to win her heart again."

The door slammed as Brooks walked out, leaving him there thinking about what he'd said.

Brooks may be right about Lydia but what he didn't know was that Lewis could be just as stubborn.

CHAPTER 10

"Miss Vaughn, can I talk to you for a moment?"

Elizabeth's voice was still quiet when she spoke but each day she seemed to be coming out of her shell a little more. Lifting her eyes from her desk, she smiled at the girl.

"Of course, Elizabeth. Is everything okay?"

Since getting her glasses, she was learning to read at an impressive pace and was like a completely different girl from when Lydia had started teaching her just a few short weeks ago.

The other kids had left already and Lydia was just going to clean up the classroom a bit before Mr. Malloy got there for her.

"My pa was hoping you'd come out for dinner tomorrow, so he could thank you for all of your help with me."

"Oh, Elizabeth, tell him that would be lovely. I'd love to have the chance to see your home." She'd met Mr. McCutcheon a few times when he'd picked Elizabeth up to walk home. He was a blacksmith in town and would sometimes come to the school to share his lunch break with Elizabeth.

The girl's smile lit up her face. "This will be so much fun. I'll tell pa to pick us up and we can walk home after school. I'm sure he'll make sure he takes you back to your room after it gets dark."

Lydia smiled at the joy in the girl's eyes. "Yes, I'm sure he will."

She watched as Elizabeth skipped toward the door to go outside. She shook her head with wonder, knowing she'd never seen the girl have a skip in her step before. She was still smiling as she went back to tidying her desk.

"Are you ready to go, Miss Vaughn?" Mr. Malloy's voice broke through the silence of the room.

She was always happy to see the kind older man when he'd show up to escort her but, deep down, she still missed seeing Lewis come through the door.

Smiling, she walked to the hook and took her jacket down, letting him help her put it on before stepping into the cold. It was getting colder each day and she knew soon the ground would be covered in a blanket of snow.

"Make sure you're bundled up. The wind is biting out there."

They made their way outside and he held her arm firmly as they went down the few steps.

After walking in silence for a while, she thought she should tell him she wouldn't need him tomorrow after school. "Mr. McCutcheon has kindly invited me for dinner tomorrow night after school. I've had the chance to eat at a few of the children's homes but hadn't gone to Elizabeth's yet. She was so excited when I told her." She smiled as she remembered.

"Ah yes, Miss Elizabeth is a sweet girl." He'd met her quite a few times since he'd been walking her to and from the schoolhouse. "It's too bad about her ma. It'll be nice for Garrett to have some company. He's been devoted to that little girl of his since his wife passed and never does anything outside of work or home."

"What happened to Elizabeth's mother, do you know?" She looked up at Mr. Malloy who was walking along beside her like they were out for a Sunday stroll. She secretly suspected he enjoyed having this time to get out for a walk and away from Edna's chatter for a while.

He was watching the street before leading her across. "From what I remember, she took ill a while back. I seem to recall hearing she was taken by pneumonia. They were a private family and didn't come out for much besides church on Sundays."

They walked a bit in silence, listening to the sounds of the late afternoon in the streets as people rushed to wherever they needed to go. "Sheriff Kinkaid might not be too happy when he hears about it, though."

She whipped her head back to look at the man who was smiling down at her. Lydia lifted her chin a little and shook her head. "Well, I don't really care what he thinks. I'm a grown woman and he holds no claim on me."

She shrugged. "Besides, it's just a meal with a student and her father. It doesn't mean the man will be courting me."

Mr. Malloy chuckled softly as they approached the hotel. "I'm sure Garrett McCutcheon would have to be blind if he doesn't see the gem across the table from him tomorrow. And I have no doubt, once the fine sheriff finds out, he's not going to be too happy."

"YOUR HOME IS LOVELY, Mr. McCutcheon. And the meal looks delicious. I'm surprised at your skills in the kitchen."

He was making a simple meal which consisted of fried ham, some potatoes, and carrots. Bread, which he confessed to buying from Mrs. Henry who sold fresh baked goods through the mercantile, was cut up and on a plate.

"Well, it's likely not the fare you're used to at the hotel with Mrs. Malloy. She's known around these parts for her cooking." He laughed as he dished the potatoes into a bowl to set on the table.

"I apologize for the wait. I'd hoped to be able to leave work early today to prepare a little better but it seemed there was no end to the people coming in needing something fixed."

"It's fine. I'm in no hurry. Besides, it's given me extra time to visit with Elizabeth. Her reading has been coming along so well." She smiled at the girl who was sitting quietly at the end of the table, beaming at the compliment.

"Thanks to you." He set the meat on the table and sat down across from her. He smiled at her and she noticed how handsome he was. His hair was black and he hadn't had time to shave since he'd picked her and Elizabeth up at the school to walk to their house.

It wasn't far to go, their house was on one of the side streets that branched off behind the blacksmith shop. Elizabeth had chatted non-stop as they'd walked home, which surprised her, and apparently her father as well. He'd looked over Elizabeth's head with his eyes wide open and shrugged at Lydia as the child continued talking about her day.

They ate the remainder of the meal in happy conversation, discussing everything about school and news around town. He was easy to talk to and she found herself laughing and having more fun than she'd had in a long time.

"I'll wash up." Elizabeth jumped up and grabbed the plates from the table. The kettle had been boiling for the hot water, so she poured it into the basin. Lydia smiled at how helpful the girl was around the house.

When she turned her head back, Garrett was watching his daughter with a smile. "I truly can't thank you enough for everything you've done for my daughter." He kept his voice low as he brought his eyes around to hers. "After her mother died, Elizabeth went into a shell and I honestly didn't think I'd ever see her smile again. The reading issue has been going on for so long and I never would've thought it was something as simple as her needing glasses."

"Well, that's my job to help kids learn and to try and be someone who they feel they can trust."

He shook his head. "No, it's more than that, what you did. Other teachers just gave up on her. You could've done the same."

She swallowed under the intense stare he was giving her.

"I guess I should be going. I don't want to impose and I have to be up early to get the school warmed up before the children arrive."

Elizabeth came over and looked up at her father as they stood up from the table. "Pa, can I come with you?"

He put his hand on the top of her head and smiled down at her. "I don't know if that's a good idea. You know the streets aren't safe at night. And besides, don't you have some reading homework?" He looked at Lydia with his eyebrows raised.

She nodded and smiled. "Yes, she does have some reading I asked her to do."

"You just stay here and I'll get Miss Vaughn back to the hotel safely. I won't be long."

He helped Lydia get her jacket on and she tied the belt tightly, then bent down to hug Elizabeth. "Thank you for the invite for dinner. I'll see you tomorrow in school."

They walked into the cold of the night air and she tucked her hands deep into her pockets. The streets were lit up with sparsely placed lamps and the lights poured from the windows of the buildings full of those who came out at night to the streets of Abilene.

She could hear loud voices and she found herself moving a bit closer to the man walking beside her. "I'm not sure I'll ever get used to the rowdiness that comes out at night in this town."

He was looking around the streets as he talked. "It never used to be like this. At least, not this bad. But the past few years have really brought out every unsavory character in the area. And now with Tom Smith gone, things are going to get bad again soon. Sheriff Kinkaid and the other men will have their hands full, that's for sure."

Hearing Lewis's name spoken out loud made her step falter slightly. Garrett reached out and steadied her with his hand on her elbow. "Careful, there's a bit of a step here."

They'd crossed the street and were stepping up onto the walkway in front of the hotel.

He kept his hand there until they got to the door and she turned to thank him. "It was a lovely evening. You really didn't have to do that for me."

He nodded his head and smiled. "Yes, I did. You've given me my Elizabeth back and I'd feared I'd lost her as surely as I lost my wife."

She didn't know what to say as they stood looking at each other on the side of the street.

"Will you be going to the Lowrey's barn dance on Saturday? It's a nice way for the community to get together to celebrate winter arriving. A few of us men will go and clean it all out to get it ready. If you'd like to go, I'd be honored if you'd let me take you."

She hesitated for a moment. She didn't want to give him any false impressions of her feelings but as she looked at him standing in the glow of the light, she realized she had truly enjoyed her visit with him tonight. It might be fun to go to a dance. She'd heard about the Lowrey's winter barn dances but had never gone.

"I'd enjoy that but I can't promise you I'm much of a dancer." She laughed as he grinned at her.

"Well, we'll have that in common then. I'll pick you up to drive out at seven o'clock. It's just outside of town."

"I'll look forward to it."

He turned to leave and she watched as he walked away. He spun back around to wave before crossing the street. She moved to go inside but felt her heart hit the ground as she saw Lewis standing across the street in front of the saloon. He pulled down on the tip of his hat in greeting, then walked away.

Seeing him standing there like that made her suddenly feel such sadness after a wonderful night.

She felt like she was missing a part of her heart and she didn't know how to move on without it.

CHAPTER 11

The warmth inside the barn was a sharp contrast to the cold outside. Lewis leaned against the wall next to the table set up with some of the pies and he let his eyes fall over the people moving around inside. The sounds of a fiddle filled the space and laughter reached his ears as couple swung around on the dance floor. Children were running around and playing while some of the older ones were dancing.

He found his eyes wandering to the doorway every time it swung open, with his heart in his throat while he waited to see who would come through. When Harold Malloy had told him Lydia had agreed to let Garrett McCutcheon take her to the Lowrey's barn dance, he'd understood how she must have felt at seeing Rose show up in town.

He'd never been the jealous type but his

stomach had been in knots ever since, trying to figure out how he could make her listen to him and see that his heart was hers. When he'd seen Garrett walking her home the other night, he'd felt an irrational urge to run over and knock the other man to the ground.

But he knew that wasn't fair. It wasn't up to him. And besides, the man wasn't doing anything wrong. Lydia was a wonderful, kind, loving woman and any man would have to be blind not to see that.

It didn't stop him from feeling angry toward the other man, though.

The door opened and he stood up straight watching to see if it was her. A swish of red velvet came through and he felt his head drop into his hands. How did she get out here? Why couldn't she just leave him alone?

Rose looked around, then lifted her hand to wave when she spotted him. The couple who came in behind her looked at him apologetically, then walked in the other direction.

"Lewis, why didn't you tell me about the dance? I would've come with you. We used to love attending balls and dances back home, remember?"

He shook his head and laughed without humor. "Honestly, Rose, I didn't figure a dance being held in a barn was exactly the kind of outing you'd enjoy."

"Well, you won't know these things if you don't

ask. Luckily for me, the Malloy's were on their way out here when I went to the hotel looking for you."

She looked around the barn filled with lights from the lanterns hanging on the walls. "Where do we put our coats?"

He put his hands out to take her coat. Even if he was annoyed that she was here, the truth was, she was a part of his past and he couldn't just ignore her. He'd have to try reasoning with her tonight and let her know any chance of them still getting married was gone.

Even if Lydia never looked his way again, Rose wasn't the type of woman who would make him happy. Being around her again had proven that to him.

Hanging her coat on a peg, he noticed the door open again. This time, the woman he'd been watching for walked through on the arm of Garrett McCutcheon. His stomach somersaulted when she turned and met his eyes.

He forgot to breathe.

Her hair was pulled up with a clip and had tendrils of curls hanging down around her ears. It may just be a simple barn dance but she'd fixed herself up prettier than any woman he'd ever witnessed at even the finest of balls back home. She was wearing a simple rose-colored skirt with a white blouse that had ruffles up around her collar.

She turned and smiled at Garrett as the man

helped her take her jacket. The young girl with them tugged at Lydia's arm and his heart flew to his throat as he watched her lurch forward on her bad leg. He moved to get to her but as soon as she started to lose her footing, Garrett reached out and steadied her. He smiled down at her, then turned and scolded the girl.

An ache he'd never felt before consumed him at the realization that the friendly relationship he'd had with Lydia was gone. She no longer needed him. It irked him because it was all just a misunderstanding, yet he felt like he'd lost his chance to prove it. He'd never felt the need to mention Rose because he'd thought she was in his past.

How was he supposed to have known she'd show up here and destroy the one chance at happiness he'd had?

"Aren't you going to ask me to dance?" Rose was beside him, pulling on his arm.

He figured he may as well do something besides stand in the corner pining for the woman who wasn't even looking his way. They got onto the dance floor and immediately he noticed Lydia up with Garrett.

"It looks like Lydia has found herself a nice-looking new beau." Rose was looking at the other couple too. Finally, she turned back to look at him.

"I guess if you're going to try winning her back, you better do something before she falls for the dark, brooding looks of the man she's dancing with."

Lewis stepped on her foot, caught completely off guard by her statement.

As they moved on the dance floor, she looked back at Lydia. "I'll never understand what you see in her compared to me but I can tell your heart's not with me anymore. When I see how you look at her, I don't think it ever was—not like that."

He swallowed hard. He wasn't sure what to say. He knew he couldn't argue with what she said because he'd realized the same thing.

"I was coming to the hotel tonight to tell you I'm leaving in the morning. I'd like to be home for Christmas, so if I leave now, there's still time. And I'm going to assume you won't be coming with me?" She phrased the last sentence as a question and she looked at him hopefully one more time.

Shaking his head, he gave her a slight smile. "I'm sorry, Rose. I belong here."

She gave a sad laugh, then nodded. "I already knew that but I had to try."

They kept dancing until the song was over, then he walked her over to the side. "Mr. Malloy has offered to give me a ride back into town once I had a chance to tell you. Maybe I'll see you again sometime." She stood up on the tips of her toes and kissed him on the cheek.

Turning, she took her coat off the hook then

walked to the doorway where Harold was already waiting.

He watched as the woman he'd thought he loved and who he'd hoped to spend his life with, walked out of his life. That part of his life was now in the past for good. No more surprises.

He stood watching the door for a moment before turning to look back into the room. Everyone was having so much fun, dancing, visiting, and enjoying the music. But his eyes found what they were looking for right away.

Sitting on a straw bale on the far wall, he saw her. He'd just said good-bye to his past. It was time to take control of his future.

❧

LEWIS STRODE across the room toward her and she coughed as she choked on the lemonade she was drinking. Elizabeth had wanted to dance with her father, so she'd come to sit down and give her leg a rest. She'd tried to ignore the couple standing by the other wall but when Rose reached up and kissed him, the pain she'd felt in her chest had been crushing.

Rose had then turned and walked outside and Lewis had spun around, seeming to find her right away. Now, he was walking toward her, and his eyes weren't moving from hers.

He put his hand out. "Would you care to dance? I promise I'll do my best to spare your toes." The smile he gave her was hopeful.

She couldn't say no without looking rude, so she nodded and put her hand into his. Instantly, that familiar warmth rushed through her body. How could he still affect her like this?

He took her in his arms, bringing his hand around her waist, and taking her other hand in his. They slowly started to move and she wasn't even sure if they were moving in time to the music or making their own.

His chest was close against hers and he held her tighter with each step she had to make on her bad leg, as though, it was natural to him. She didn't even think he realized he was doing it.

"Rose is leaving tomorrow."

He said the words clearly and his chest rumbled against hers as he spoke into her ear.

"What? Why?" She couldn't understand why Rose was leaving.

He pulled back a bit to look down at her. "Because I told you, Rose was from my past. Just because she still thought we had a future, didn't mean that's what I wanted. She's not the woman who has my heart."

She could feel her legs start to give out and she was thankful he was holding her up. Was he saying...?

"Lewis! They need you over at the Alamo. Some hothead is in there shooting things up, laughing about how there's no one to stop them from having their guns now." One of the other men who worked with Lewis had run up behind him.

Lewis closed his eyes tightly, then stepped back. He still held her hand in his. "I guess we'll have to finish this talk another time."

He spun and raced out the door behind the other man, leaving her with nothing to do but pray they'd actually get the chance.

CHAPTER 12

She pulled her jacket up tightly and put her arm around Elizabeth's shoulders as she leaned against her for warmth. The night had gotten colder with the first snow finally making its way from the skies. The flakes were large and fluffy, landing on the backs of the horses pulling the wagon before melting.

When the dance had ended, everyone went to the wagons and now made a line snaking their way back toward town. The snorting of the horses and the jingling of the reins sounded louder in the crisp, cold air around them. The snow crunched beneath the horse's hooves and they could see their breath as they spoke.

"I think someone might have fallen asleep." She smiled at Garrett and he looked over to see Elizabeth slouching against Lydia.

"She had a great time tonight. It was wonderful seeing her having fun like that again." He looked back at the road ahead.

"It was a nice evening. I can't thank you enough for taking me. I've always wanted to go to one of the Lowrey barn dances but had never had the chance." She'd enjoyed herself tonight, as much as someone could while worrying about a man who'd run off to break up a gunfight while still recovering from his last bullet wound.

He turned and smiled again. He really was a good-looking man and she could tell he had a kind heart. He was the kind of man she should be falling in love with.

Yet, all she could think of was the night Lewis had driven her home in the wagon and stopped to kiss her.

"So, Sheriff Kinkaid didn't seem too happy to see you at the dance with me." He was grinning now and she couldn't tell if the sparkle she was seeing in his eyes was from the reflection of the snow or something else.

She shrugged. "I'm sure he wouldn't care one way or another." She tried to make her voice sound convincing.

He laughed softly. "Lydia, I've been in love before and I'd recognize the signs anywhere. And I'm not the kind of man to step on another's toes.

But I'll tell you now, if Lewis Kinkaid doesn't figure out what he's doing and make things right with you, I might not be so inclined to step back."

"You're a good man, Mr. McCutcheon. And I have no doubt someday, another woman will come along and show you how to love again."

He nodded but kept his eyes straight ahead. "I'd appreciate if you call me Garrett. Mr. McCutcheon was my father. As for me loving again, I don't know if I've got it in me. Everything I have left is for my little girl here." He turned and smiled down at his daughter again.

Lydia was sure she'd never seen a man who loved his daughter more than he did.

She wished she could offer him more but she knew her heart wasn't ready either. And after tonight, she was even more confused than ever.

"SHERIFF KINKAID, I'm going to be a wiser man." Mary ran up to him as he approached the schoolhouse. The snow was coming down again but the day was warm enough for the children to be playing outside.

"Do you mean a wise man, Mary?" He smiled down at the rosy cheeks and serious upturned face as she looked at him.

"Yes. I wanted to be Mary because that's my name. But Miss Vaughn says that Elizabeth will be Mary. Who ever heard of Mary having glasses?"

Lewis chuckled to himself at the words that came out of the little girl's mouth. She was always guaranteed to make you smile.

"Hello, Lewis." He lifted his head at Lydia's voice. He'd thought she'd still be inside the classroom getting things ready for her afternoon lessons. She was smiling at him, or perhaps she'd overheard Mary's conversation, but he was relieved to see she was at least willing to talk to him.

Since he'd run out of the dance the other evening, he hadn't had a chance to see her. One of the men involved in the gunfight had been wanted for another crime, so he'd been chosen to escort the man to Topeka. He'd just got back this morning and he'd gone to get cleaned up a bit before coming to see her.

"Mary was just telling me she gets to be a wise man." He offered her a smile.

Lydia nodded and reached out to pull the little girl's hat down to cover her ears from the cold. "Yes, I think she'll be a fine wise man for our nativity play. We're going to start practicing this afternoon."

"And Elizabeth and Pete are going to be married." Mary brought her gloved hand up to cover her mouth as she snickered behind it.

Lydia shook her head and laughed. "Now, Mary,

you run along and play. Lunch break will be over soon and we have a lot of practicing to do this afternoon."

She looked back at Lewis and shrugged. "Elizabeth and Pete will be playing the parts of Mary and Joseph. Much to Mary's chagrin, since she figures the part of Mary is destined to be hers."

"I can't wait to see what you put together. When will the performance be?"

"I've spoken to Reverend Hall about having the children perform the nativity play and sing a few Christmas carols at the Christmas Eve service. He was so excited about the idea."

They started walking around the schoolyard and a few of the children ran by, stopping to say hello to him. Many of them had known him a long time and when he'd been coming to the school with Lydia, he'd gotten to know them all.

"I was hoping we could have the chance to finish the talk we were having the other night when we were interrupted." He'd been trying to figure out how to say it, so he figured blurting it out was likely the easiest.

She stopped and looked up at him. "I'd like that. I've had some time to think and I realize I wasn't being fair to you. I should have given you a chance to explain, instead of just assuming the worst. It wasn't right."

He stood staring at her stunned, unsure what to

say. He'd been prepared to beg her if he had to and she'd just caught him off guard. After the amount of time he'd known this woman, he should have realized nothing could surprise him.

Her cheeks were red from the cold in the air and so was the tip of her nose. With the way she was smiling at him, he was forcing himself not to reach out and pull her into his arms.

"I appreciate that. But I know it looked bad, having Rose show up like that. There are just some things in my past that, in my mind, are meant to stay there. And I assumed that included my engagement. I truly didn't realize she still thought we'd be going through with our marriage. I never would've lied to you on purpose."

She looked past him at a few of the boys who were running past and throwing snowballs at each other. "Boys, be careful you don't hit any of the girls who aren't playing."

Finally, she looked back at him, her blue eyes staring deeply into his. It was trying every ounce of strength he had not to kiss her.

"I know that. And, I shouldn't have let my own insecurities get in the way. I've known you a long time and I know the kind of man you are."

He brought his hand out to take hers between them. The white of the snow in the tree behind her highlighted the brown hair that peeked out from the warm hat she wore. They both wore gloves, but as soon as his fingers touched hers, he felt the heat burning through the fabric.

"I was actually coming here to say that Mr. Malloy can't make it to pick you up from school today. So I volunteered, even though he said he didn't know if that was a good idea. He's sure protective of you." He wanted to pull her closer but the children were all running around them, oblivious to the scene playing out.

"He's a kind man. He's just worried about me getting hurt."

He kept his eyes on hers and could feel his heart clench at the thought of someone thinking he could do that to her. "Are you afraid of that too?" His voice was low and his pulse picked up as he waited to hear her answer.

She just looked back at him, not saying anything. Finally, she swallowed and licked her lips. "I don't think so."

He wanted to prove to her she never had to be worried about that. As long as he was breathing, he'd do whatever he could to prove it to her.

Suddenly, something hit him on the back of the shoulder. Lydia's lips started to tremble as she fought to hold back her laughter.

He raised his eyebrow and turned slowly. The boys who'd been throwing snowballs all stood in shock, unsure what was going to happen. A couple of them dropped the snow they had in their hands, while the others stood with their hands still out as though, they'd been struck frozen and couldn't move.

"You boys hit Sheriff Kinkaid...you're in so much trouble! He's going to get his cuffs and haul you all away to the gallows!"

He cringed at Mary's words. They'd come out hushed but full of disbelief. Honestly, where did she hear these things she was always repeating at the wrong times?

Bending over slowly, he grabbed a handful of snow and formed it into a ball. Pete looked afraid to move, unsure how this was going to play out.

Pulling his arm back, he fired it right at the boy who'd thrown the snowball at him. Immediately, the children realized they weren't in trouble and, in fact, Sheriff Kinkaid had just challenged them to a snowball fight.

He ran around chasing after them until a stray snowball flew and hit Lydia on the side of her face. Everyone stood still this time, even him. He started to walk toward her to make sure she was all right when she turned slightly and bent to pick up snow into her hand.

"You wouldn't."

She tipped her head and appeared to be chewing her lip as she contemplated it. Before he could move, she'd thrown it with surprising accuracy, covering his own face with the wet powder.

If he hadn't already known, he was sure at this moment the beautiful woman in front of him had just stolen his heart.

CHAPTER 13

"So Mary, how did the practice go?"

Lydia smiled as she lifted her head to see the man who'd just walked in the door. The children were getting their coats on to leave for the day and Mary was sitting on the floor right in front of the door as she struggled to get her worn boots on.

"It wasn't nothing that I was wise about. I don't even know how to be so wise." She was shaking her head as she fought with the laces on her boot, not even looking up at Lewis. Lydia watched from behind her desk as he crouched down and helped the little girl do up her laces.

"Well, I'm sure a smart young lady like you will figure out how to be wise." He gave the child a wink, then stood up and put his hand out to help her up too.

"Yes, I suppose you're right. And anyway, I get to sing some of the words to a song all by myself. Miss Vaughn says I have a beautiful voice. Pa says I have the voice of an angel but my baby brother cries when I sing, so I don't think he likes it so much."

Lydia brought her hand up to stop the laugh that threatened to burst forth as she watched the shocked expression on Lewis's face. She'd become so accustomed to Mary's chatter that she sometimes didn't even notice. But Lewis was standing with his mouth partway open and eyebrows raised as he tried to keep up with what the little girl was saying.

"I got to go now, Sheriff. Thanks for tying my boots." And just like that, the child raced out the door, leaving him standing and watching her go. Lydia stood to go to the door and say her good-byes to the rest of the children, then closed the door behind them.

When she turned back, he was slowly shaking his head. "She must be full of wisdom to share with you all day."

She laughed as she pulled her coat from the hook. "You have no idea."

He helped her put her coat over her shoulders, keeping his hands in place when he got the jacket on. Pressing slightly, he turned her to face him.

"I've missed you, Lydia. I didn't realize how much you'd become a part of my life."

His voice sounded strained, like he was fighting a battle he couldn't control.

"I missed you too." Her voice was barely above a whisper as his eyes held hers in their depths. His hand came up to brush her cheek and, somehow, she ended up right against him. She realized she'd leaned into him and he was holding her firm.

Hearing him swallow, her gaze moved to his lips. A soft groan came from his chest and his mouth came down on hers. He kissed her with an urgency she'd never felt as his hand tangled in her hair then moved down her neck.

Her insides were turning in circles with every touch he made on her skin. Finally, when she was sure she'd faint from the overwhelming sensations she was feeling, he pulled his head back.

His gaze looked down longingly at hers as he brought his fingers up to trace her lips. "I don't know what you've done to me, Lydia Vaughn, but I do know, I can't live without you. Will you marry me?"

She stood as frozen to the spot as the boys had been earlier in the snow. This was something she'd dreamed of happening and with the man she'd only imagined could love her.

He was standing in front of her asking him to be his wife. Could she be enough to make him happy?

Nodding, she finally choked out her answer. "Yes, I'll marry you."

He lifted her up and spun her around the room.

"Lewis, let me go!" She laughed at the happiness she could see on his face.

He set her down gently then looked at her, suddenly serious. "Never." He shook his head for emphasis.

"Don't say anything to anyone until I have a chance to speak to Brooks. You know he'll likely have something to say."

Lewis shrugged. "I'm not afraid of your brother. He's a lot of smoke, without the fire. Besides, then maybe he can stop worrying about you so much."

They walked outside and he helped her down the steps. Everything was slippery with the layer of snow on the ground, so she had to be sure to hold tight to the railing when she used the stairs.

She tried not to let the familiar feelings of embarrassment consume her when someone had to help her. Especially someone she desperately wanted to see her as perfect. She knew Lewis accepted her as she was but even though she outwardly showed self-confidence, she still struggled every day to believe she wasn't damaged in other's eyes.

They made their way up the street, easily finding their way back to the comfortable camaraderie they'd shared before.

"Sheriff Kinkaid. I have a telegram here for you." The young clerk from the post office ran out as they walked by. He was tall and lanky and kept his hair slicked back on his head. The suspenders he wore looked like they were stretched as far as they could go and as he nodded in her direction, his cheeks turning red. He, obviously, was nervous around women.

"Thanks, Taggart." Lewis took the paper from the man's hands, then read it. She watched his expression, noticing the way his jaw clenched firmly. Her stomach did another quick flip as she realized the man in front of her, with the strong jawline and soft lips, would soon be her husband.

He swore softly, making her tip her head to the side. "Pardon me? What could possibly be so bad that you'd use language like that in front of a lady?" She wasn't really mad. In truth, growing up with a brother like Brooks, she'd heard her share of language not meant for a lady's ears.

He looked at her apologetically. "It would appear my parents are coming for a visit over Christmas."

She smiled widely. "Well, that's wonderful! You haven't seen them in years."

This time he tipped his head sideways. "And why do you suppose that would be? I've told you I didn't exactly leave on good terms with my father. He's coming here for no other reason than to try and make me go back home."

"Can't you believe your parents might be coming to visit their son?"

He shook his head. "My mother will be coming to visit but for my father, there will be an underlying reason. He doesn't do anything unless it's for money or some kind of gain for himself."

They were still standing on the street and the evening cold was starting to seep in. She shivered but sensed he wasn't ready to move yet.

He looked at her and clenched his eyes tight for a few seconds before opening them again and piercing her gaze with his stare. "I need to tell you something else."

Her heart plummeted to her feet. Now, what could he possibly be hiding from her?

His throat moved as he swallowed hard and he leaned back against a hitching post on the street. "My family has money."

She raised an eyebrow at him. That was it? "I already knew that, Lewis. That's never been a secret. You might not talk about it but I've always known."

He shook his head. "No, it hasn't. But I don't think you realize just how much money my family has. And how important society and order means to my father. He's never been happy with my decision to walk away from all of that. Money and prestige mean everything to him and when he comes here, I don't see it being for a friendly visit."

She had a sudden sense of foreboding. If Lewis felt this way about his own father, what must the man be like? Surely any man that would have a son as good and decent as Lewis couldn't really be that bad.

Could he?

CHAPTER 14

"Elizabeth, this is the third day in a row you've forgotten your glasses. You must try to remember them tomorrow."

She kept her eyes on the young girl in front of her, trying to see what was really going on. Elizabeth had been acting strangely for a few days and now it was starting to affect her schoolwork. Without her glasses, she was having trouble keeping up with everything.

She hadn't wanted to embarrass the girl in front of the class, so she'd called her up to the front to speak with her.

Elizabeth kept her hands crossed in front of her with her head down. "I'm sorry ma'am. I'll be sure to remember them tomorrow."

Lydia watched her walk back to her desk, then turned her head when the door at the back of the room opened. She smiled at the figure who stomped through the door in a swirl of snow. His head was down and he was carrying something that was giving him some trouble. Pete jumped up and went to give him a hand.

"Sorry to interrupt class but I wanted to bring this by right away to make sure it met Miss Vaughn's approval. I figured it'd be nice to have it for practice today." Lewis was grinning at her like a schoolboy himself as he held up the large manger he'd made for the play. Lydia had mentioned she didn't really have any props and immediately he'd volunteered to help.

Mrs. Malloy had gone through old linens she had and they'd worked out some costumes for the play. And each of the children looked around home to see what they could find. Now, it was looking like this would be the most popular event of the season.

It was all up to the children who were incredibly excited about the play they were putting on for the town.

Everyone in the room was even more worked up after seeing the prop Lewis had brought so she knew it would be impossible to try doing any lessons.

"All right, class. Since Sheriff Kinkaid has been so kind and worked so hard on this manger for our play, perhaps we should let him sit in on our practice today. What do you think?"

Everyone shouted excitedly for him to stay.

He worked with Pete to set the manger up at the front. When he was done, he came over and smiled down at her. "Well, how does it look?"

She looked over at the wooden prop and tilted her head as though she was thinking about it. "It'll do, I suppose."

She laughed at his feigned look of hurt that she wasn't being more enthusiastic.

"But you do realize, you're going to have to carry it to the church now?"

He nodded and gave a shrug. "I know. I wanted you to have it to practice today, though."

She could feel her whole body warm up at his thoughtfulness.

"Plus, I needed some reason to be able to come and see my fiancée," he'd leaned sideways to whisper in her ear, with his arms crossed in front of him.

"Lewis! Shhh...you don't want someone overhearing."

He grumbled. "Well if your stubborn oaf of a brother would get into town, we could tell everyone. Usually he's like a bee under my britches, always in the way, but now, when I'd actually like him to be around, he's decided to stay put at the farm."

"They're coming in for the service and to see the play on Christmas Eve. I'm going to go back home with them for Christmas. I still wish you'd reconsider and come out with your parents to spend Christmas with us."

He'd always planned to spend Christmas Day at Brooks and Fiona's but when his parents decided to come, he'd changed his mind. He'd said he wouldn't submit everyone else to that torture.

He moved forward to help Mary get her fabric tied to her hair. "No, we'll wait and perhaps the following day we can get everyone together to tell them the news."

"What's your news?" Mary was looking up at them with bright eyes.

"Mary, what have I told you about listening to grown-up conversations?" Lydia shooed the little girl to her position.

"All right, class, let's show Sheriff Kinkaid what we've learned."

"JUST TRUST ME. Keep your eyes closed and I'll lead you."

The sound of her laughter made his heart swell. It was a sound he'd never get tired of hearing.

"Lewis, this is silly. I can't walk without seeing where I'm going."

He was holding her by the elbow and leading her along the edge of the street. They'd walked for a while until he told her to close her eyes so he could show her a surprise.

Their feet crunched in the snow and as they made their way along. He could see she was having trouble because she couldn't gauge the balance she needed to take each step. He looked around to see if anyone was in the vicinity then reached down and put his arms behind her legs, lifting her swiftly into his arms.

She squealed as her feet left the ground. "Lewis, put me down! Someone will see!"

Her arms had come up around his neck and she was clinging on for dear life.

"There's no one around. We're on the street behind the school and there's not a soul in sight. Besides, we're almost there."

He walked a few more steps, savoring the feeling of Lydia in his arms. She was resting her head against his shoulder and he could smell the soap she used for washing as he placed his nose near her hair.

Finally reaching the destination, he reached out and opened the door, then placed her feet back onto the floor. He stood up behind her, holding her by the shoulders as he looked around.

"Okay, open your eyes."

Her head moved slowly as she looked around the room. Finally, she stepped away from him and looked up with her eyebrows furrowed. "Where are we?"

"It's our house."

He watched the expression on her face as she scanned the small room again. He wished he could give her a mansion but on his salary, this was the best he could do. It was a comfortable home and he'd thought it'd be perfect since it was so close to the school. He hoped they could spend their first years of married life there together.

"But..." She was shaking her head in confusion.

"I told you awhile back, I'd been thinking of getting my own house in town. I figured now was as good a time as any since we'd be getting married soon. I don't think living in a hotel is best for a newlywed couple."

She walked over and ran her fingers over the table top. The house was still furnished. The family who'd lived here previously had obviously moved on and didn't want to drag everything with them. She turned and took everything in and when she looked back at him, he noticed the wetness in her eyes.

He walked over and put his hands on her shoulders, pulling her in close. His finger came up to wipe away the tear that had made its way out. "I didn't mean to make you cry." Seeing the tears, his heart lurched.

She shook her head and pushed her lips into a firm line. "No, it's just...it's too much."

He almost laughed at the expression on her face. The fact that she thought this was too much made him love her even more. This house was nice but it wasn't as big or grand as she deserved.

There was only the one large room, with a smaller one off the side for a bedroom. But in here was a table and chairs, a stand for washing, and a long sideboard by the stove. Next to the fireplace were two chairs and a bench along the wall. She walked into the kitchen and placed her hands on the stove. "I can imagine making our meals on this stove."

When she lifted her face and smiled, it tugged at his heart. "I'll look forward to being able to spend our days together here and as much as I love Mrs. Malloy's cooking, I'd much rather be eating yours."

She turned and walked into the doorway off the kitchen. In the small room, there was a bed and a chest for their clothes. He wondered if her insides were in as much turmoil as his were as he imagined spending his life here with her.

Turning to face him, she walked back and smiled up at him.

"It's perfect."

He reached out to tuck a piece of her hair into her hat. It was chilly inside the house without the stove going, so he was glad they'd kept their outdoor clothes on. It was starting to get later in the day and the rooms were dim without the lanterns that would keep them lit.

"I can't wait to start our lives together." His

voice sounded strained to his own ears, as he lowered his head to gently place his lips on hers. He knew he had to stop before he was no longer able to. Pulling his head back, he traced his fingers along the lips that were still parted.

She smiled and reached up to hold his hand, pressing it to her cheek. "Thank you."

As he looked into the eyes smiling back at him, he knew he was the one who should be thanking her.

CHAPTER 15

"It's a pleasure to meet you, Lydia." The small woman nodded and curtsied as she took her hand in hers before sitting in the chair her husband was holding out for her.

Lewis's mother was stunning.

She was petite, with porcelain white skin, and brown hair that seemed to have a shade of every other color shining through in it. There wasn't a strand out of place, held up on her head with the most beautiful clip she'd ever seen. It was full of blue jewels that matched her silk dress perfectly. Lydia self-consciously reached up to tuck stray pieces of hair back into the clip she wore that blended in with the brown of her own hair.

"So, Lewis tells us you're the schoolteacher in town. That must be a very rewarding job." Lewis's father sat down across from her and suddenly she got the impression she was being tested. The way he was looking at her and scanning around the room with disdain, she already knew she would never measure up.

To him, she was a symbol of this dusty, uncivilized cow town out west that was no place for his son.

"Yes, it's a wonderful job and I love the children." She smiled at his mother who seemed genuinely happy to be meeting the woman her son was introducing them to. They'd already decided to tell his parents tonight that they were going to marry and would tell Brooks when he came in for the play tomorrow evening.

"You live on your own, in this town?" He waved his hands around the room as he shook his head slightly.

"Well, yes. As the schoolteacher, I need to be in town. I have a room that's provided for teachers at the Merchants Hotel."

Lewis's father looked at him with an eyebrow raised. "The same hotel you're staying at?"

Lewis was sitting back in his chair with his arms crossed in front of him. As soon as his father had stepped into the room, even after not seeing each other for years, she'd sensed his anger. He wasn't prepared to let his father make him feel bad.

"Yes, Father, the same hotel. Her brother asked

me to keep an eye on her while she was in town and that's what I did."

"So, you felt a duty to look after her."

Lewis stared at his father for a long time before answering. "As I would with anyone in this town. I'm a sheriff, so that's what I do."

His father shrugged. "Yes, you keep reminding me. The job that's so worthwhile, it's keeping you from your duties back home."

"Lawrence, that's enough." Lewis's mother tapped him on the arm. "I haven't seen my son in a long time. I won't let you ruin this visit."

They were dining at the finest restaurant in Abilene which really wasn't fancy by any of the standards the Kinkaids would be used to back home. But the Regency Hotel was the best in town and it where Lewis had arranged for his parents to stay while they were here. The restaurant downstairs was the one used for business meetings and the more polished of society to enjoy.

Lydia had never felt more uncomfortable in her life. She'd met Lewis's father earlier, while his mother was having a rest in her room. He'd brought him by the schoolyard at lunch time when she'd been outside with the children. They'd only arrived and his father had wanted a tour of Abilene.

But sitting at this table, the tension was thicker than gravy. She felt bad for his mother who seemed so happy to see her son. But his father wouldn't budge in his arrogance and anger over Lewis not coming home to live the life his father believed was his due.

"I heard about Tom Smith being killed on duty. And that was after he'd already had a couple of assassination attempts. He's not the first law man in this area to be killed. Why would you want to stay here and risk your life like this? Is it just to get back at me and prove you don't need your family money?"

Lydia cringed as his father brought the conversation around to Lewis's choices again. Lewis was taking a sip of his coffee but he met his father's eyes, then slowly put the cup down on the table. Lydia's heart was beating so hard, she was sure they could all see it outside her white blouse. How could they tell him about their marriage if he was this unhappy about Lewis being here?

The muscles in Lewis's jaw moved as he fought to control his anger.

"I have plenty of reasons to want to stay here, none of which have anything to do with you. It's been no secret I have no desire to live the society life you have set out for me. If you could have just accepted that, maybe things might've been different. But you couldn't see that, could you?"

She was scared to look at his father, knowing he was not going to be happy with the direction this conversation was headed. "And now, I have no intentions of leaving here. Not so long as Lydia's here."

She could feel both of his parents' eyes land on her. Swallowing hard, she glanced at his mom and offered a nervous smile. This was never how she'd imagined this moment in her life to be.

"Lydia and I are going to be married. And the sooner, the better."

His mother's eyes lit up with happiness but she could almost feel the anger palpitating from his father. He'd just found out his son not only wasn't going to be coming home but he was marrying a woman far below his perceived station.

"I think we need to discuss this, son." Lewis's father looked at her with a solemn expression. "Nothing against you Lydia, I'm sure you're a fine woman. But Lewis has responsibilities and he can't just walk away from those. No matter what he may think. And one of those responsibilities was marrying Rose Parker. It's been arranged between the families for years."

"Father...this isn't up for discussion. Rose and I have reached an agreement and she's gone home."

"Yes, well, the last I'd heard, she'd come out here. She sent me a telegram letting me know you were rejecting her and that you fancied some drab schoolteacher but I'd never believed it could be true."

So that's why his parents had suddenly felt the

urge to pay him a visit. Rose had sent them a message when she first got here.

Lewis stood up quickly, his chair scraping the floor loudly.

"I won't let you insult, Lydia. If you want to talk about this, we'll go out to the lobby away from the women."

He wasn't leaving any room for argument and his father must have sensed it because he planted his lips in a firm line, then stood to follow him from the room.

Lydia looked down at her tea that was no longer steaming, afraid to meet his mother's eyes. She could feel tears threatening and she wished she could just go anywhere else but here.

She jumped as Anne Kinkaid reached out and gently placed her hand on hers. She looked up into the kind eyes staring at her. Now she knew where Lewis got his eyes from as she realized the depth of compassion in her eyes.

"I apologize for my husband. He's always been hotheaded and, unfortunately, he has a son just like him. They've locked horns on more than one occasion and I've just had to learn to look the other way. I have no doubt they love each other but Lawrence is so set in his ways he has a hard time seeing past them."

Lydia swallowed and nodded her head. "I'd never try to keep Lewis from something he's meant to be doing. I really believe this is what he enjoys and I worry about him just as much as you both do, I'm sure."

They sat a moment longer until Lydia finally decided she was ready to go back to the hotel. If Lewis and his father wanted to stand around arguing, she didn't want any part of it. Lewis's mother agreed, so they stood to go to the lobby. As they got closer, they could hear the voices raised in anger.

"No, you have a duty to this family. You can't just walk away like you did and not think you have responsibilities."

"My life is here, in Abilene. And wherever Lydia and I decide to make it. That's not up for discussion."

"You're going to give everything up? All of the money, everything, to stay here and marry a woman who is crippled?"

The air felt like it had been knocked out of her lungs. Over the years, she'd faced the stares and heard the comments whispered behind hands. But she'd never heard a word so full of hatred as she'd just heard. She stumbled and had to put her hand out to brace herself against the doorway.

Lewis had grabbed his father by the collar and pushed him against the wall, still oblivious to the women who'd come out.

"Don't you ever say those words again." The

anger could be felt where she was standing as he hissed the words in his father's face.

"Oh..." His mother's voice finally broke through the fury Lewis was consumed by and he turned, slowly letting his father's feet touch the ground again. Immediately, he looked at Lydia, and she could see his eyes fill with pain.

"Lydia..." He came to her, taking her hands in his.

"Lewis, I'd like to go home now."

She'd never been so humiliated and hurt in her life and now she'd caused a rift in Lewis's family she didn't think could be repaired.

Not only that, she just realized that all her fears about not being good enough for him weren't just her own silly thoughts.

She knew, now, others had believed it too.

CHAPTER 16

"Here, Pete, set it over here on the straw, then put some inside."

Pete had been helping with the setup of some of the bigger items for the play while the younger children raced around finding places for some of the smaller props.

It was Christmas Eve and the play was tonight. Excitement was running high with all the children eager to show the community the wonderful play they'd been working on.

Lydia wished she could still feel the joy she had in the beginning. This was a day she'd been so excited about when she'd started planning this Christmas Eve show for the people in the community. She knew Abilene wasn't the nicest place to live but there were still good people in the town who she knew would enjoy what the children were doing.

But, today, all she kept hearing in her mind were the words Lewis's father had spewed, leaving her feeling like she'd been dunked in cold water and left lying naked on the ground. All of the feelings of insecurity she'd fought through, to let herself believe she could be good enough for Lewis. Then it had all been thrown back into the front of her mind with that one question she'd had the misfortune to hear spoken out loud.

"Miss Vaughn, are you all right?" Mary's voice broke into her thoughts as she sat in the front pew of the church, her arms hugging herself for comfort. Every prop had been moved here, ready for the show. She needed to focus and get it set up so the children could go home and have dinner before the play.

Mary sat down beside her, took her hand in her small one and looked up at her with her bright blue eyes. "I'm so glad you came to town, Miss Vaughn."

Struggling against the lump that suddenly formed in her throat, she smiled down at the little girl. "I am too, Mary."

"None of the other teachers ever wanted to stay here. And we've never been able to do a play for Christmas!"

No matter what, at least Lydia knew she could do the teaching job she loved so much. The children all accepted her for who she was and appreciated what she did.

Deciding it was time to stop feeling sorry for herself long enough to let these children have the perfect play they'd worked so hard for, she nodded and stood up, pulling Mary with her. "Let's get this all finished up here so you can go home and eat. Tonight's a big night. You have to put this play on for the people of the town, then get home before Santa arrives!"

Mary's squeal brought a smile to her heart as the little girl jumped up to run and finish.

Once the manger was in the right place and everything else was set where the children placed them, she bundled them up and shooed them out the door to go home and get ready for tonight.

Holding the door as Pete walked out, the last one to leave, she started to push it closed. Standing on the step was Lewis's father.

"Can I come in and speak with you for a moment, Miss Vaughn?" The late afternoon air was cold and there were a few small flakes of snow falling around his shoulders.

She stepped back and let him inside, closing the door behind him.

He went over by the wood stove and held his hands out, rubbing them together for warmth. She followed but stayed back enough that she wouldn't have to be too close to him.

He finally turned to face her. "I wanted to apologize for my words last night. I was out of line and what I said was in anger. Not at you but at the stubbornness of my son who can't seem to understand my position. It's no excuse, though, for the harshness of my words and I hope you can see it in your heart to forgive me."

She wanted to forgive him, knowing he was the father of the man she loved. But how could she ever erase what she'd heard?

"I know I'm not the woman you'd have chosen for Lewis. I can't compare to a woman like Rose Parker. But I love your son. And I only want him to be happy, so I promise to do whatever I can to see that he is."

He nodded, then reached inside his jacket, pulling out a pouch that was larger than his hand. He held it in his hand and looked at her.

"I thought you were likely the kind of woman who'd understand. Who'd be able to see that Lewis might believe he's happy here now but, the truth is, that he's just running away from his duties back home as he's done in the past. He's trying to make a point and he's made it. But the time will come when he will resent what he's had to give up and he'll realize what he's done. I'm trying to spare you the pain of when that happens."

He reached out with his hand for her to take the pouch. Letting him place it in her hand, she wondered what he was giving her.

"I'm offering you a chance to help him. If you

love him, as you say, let him come home where he belongs. He's had his chance to run away and prove his point but if he stays here, he's giving up a lot of money and prestige he'll never get back." He tipped his head toward the heavy pouch she held in her hand.

"That bag has some money that I think you'll see is more than fair. It's for you. I'm asking you to take this money and do what you know in your heart is right."

She stood facing him, unable to speak. The weight of the bag seemed to be getting heavier with each passing second.

Without another word, he pushed past her and walked out the door.

Sitting down on the chair by the door, she fought to get her breathing under control as her entire body shook.

She knew Lewis would be there to pick her up soon. What would she tell him?

Should she?

And worse yet, was what his father said, true?

❧

LEWIS STILL SHOOK with anger every time he thought about what had happened last night. His father had crossed a line that he wasn't prepared to let him get away with.

He'd walked Lydia home but she'd barely said a word. He knew she was in shock as much as he was and it tore at his heart to see how upset she was.

Lewis had assured her that what his father said wasn't at all what he himself had ever thought as he tried to apologize for the unkind words he hadn't even spoken.

Then he'd helped her and the children bring all of the props down to the church earlier today along with Garrett McCutcheon in his wagon. The children had all been so excited and full of energy but Lydia seemed like the life had been drained from her.

And Lewis knew it'd been obvious to the other man who was helping too. He'd been shooting looks between the two of them while they worked, noting the tension. Lewis had pretended not to notice and tried to act like everything was fine.

But something had changed in her last night. And he was desperately trying to figure out how to fix it.

"Are you ready to go?" He'd walked inside the church and gave a low whistle as he looked around at the decorating she and the children had put together. She was sitting on one of the pews facing the front and hadn't turned yet to face him.

Walking up the aisle to where she sat, the sound of his boots echoed in the empty church as the floor creaked under every step he took. He sat beside her, noticing she hadn't even looked at him. She was just staring ahead, holding her hands crossed in her lap.

"Lydia, are you all right?"

She gave a slight smile, then nodded. "Yes, just having a moment to rest before tonight. It's going to be busy." She turned to look at him and he immediately recognized sadness in her eyes.

How could he fix this? He took one of her hands in his and turned slightly so he was facing her. "About my father..."

She shook her head and put her other hand up to stop him. "I don't want to talk about it. Or him. Tonight is Christmas Eve and this is an important night for all of the children. They've worked hard for this, so I don't want to be thinking of anything else."

He nodded, understanding. "Well, I've asked him to leave as soon as Christmas is over. I will be coming to spend the day with you at Brooks and Fiona's. I don't owe him anything more than that."

She shrugged and it tore at his heart, seeing the hurt in the movement. "You should stay with your mother. It isn't fair to not have Christmas with her. You're her son and she's obviously been missing you."

"Well, I've told them they'd be more than welcome out at your brother's for the day but I have no doubt they'll decline that offer."

She was avoiding looking at him and he

wondered what she was thinking. Finally, she stood and turned toward him but he couldn't see any hint of what she was feeling in her eyes at all.

"I better get going. I have to be back here in a couple of hours and I'd like to have a rest first."

He could tell she wasn't herself but he didn't want to push her. As soon as his parents were gone, he'd spend the rest of his life making up to her for the horrible words spoken by his father.

CHAPTER 17

She peeked out from behind the makeshift curtains they'd hung on the rope at the front of the church. It seemed as though the entire community had shown up, filling the church with happy chatter while they waited for the children to start.

She gasped as she saw Lewis's parents sitting with him near the back. He was sitting beside his mother, ignoring the man beside them. Lawrence Kinkaid's eyes met hers and she knew he was silently waiting to see what she'd decided.

The fact that she hadn't returned the money to him right away had obviously led him to believe he'd won. She should march over right now and give it back to him but something was fighting inside her and she still didn't know what to do.

Not that she wanted the money. That was never

the question. She had no use for the money he'd given her and, in fact, hadn't even opened the pouch to see how much was there.

No, her struggle was with the words he'd spoken. *Would* Lewis end up hating it here? Would he resent her because he'd given up everything he could have had?

Even though his father had apologized and Lewis had assured her the words hadn't been spoken in truth, she knew her limitations. She wasn't perfect. And maybe Lewis deserved someone who was.

Every fear she'd had since childhood had been blowing around in her head and she'd never felt so confused.

She'd told Lewis when he dropped her off earlier that she'd come back to the church with Brooks when he arrived and that she'd like to just have Christmas at home with her brother. She'd asked him not to say anything about getting married yet.

She knew if Brooks ever caught wind of what had happened last night, he'd be apt to spend the rest of his days in a prison cell after he was done with Lewis's father.

"We're all ready to go, Miss Vaughn," Pete whispered across to her, so she pulled on one side of the curtain while he opened the other.

The clapping and gasps of happiness from the

crowd had the entire cast of children smiling as they started going through the lines they'd rehearsed.

The church was warm against the cold of the snow coming down outside and everyone was in the spirit of the season, enjoying the show before they headed home to celebrate with family and loved ones.

As she stood off to the side, helping some of the younger children if they forgot their lines, she happened to turn her head and saw Lewis watching her. He smiled at her and she thought he looked somber as though the smile had a sadness to it.

Her eyes kept finding his and she wished she could just go and tell him she didn't care about anything his father said. She wanted to be selfish and not worry about whether he'd end up being unhappy or not.

Finally, the play finished with a flourish of standing ovations from the crowd and loud applause that threatened to shatter the windows of the church.

Pulling the curtains closed, she hugged the children to her as they all jumped up and down with happiness.

"You were all wonderful! You should be proud."

"I didn't even forget none of my lines, Miss Vaughn. I was the bestest wise man ever." She didn't even bother correcting Mary who was still excited from the show she'd put on.

"Now, children, remember. We need to push all the props to the back of the church until we can get them cleaned up next week before anyone leaves tonight."

They all worked together, while the parents and families waited to take them home. As she watched, she noticed the way Elizabeth was blushing and talking every time Pete came near her. She smiled to herself as she noticed Pete was being extra nice to Elizabeth too.

Her eyebrows came together as she looked at the girl more closely.

"Elizabeth, where are your glasses?" Lydia couldn't believe the girl had forgotten them again and that she'd only just noticed. "Has something happened to them?" She was beginning to believe the girl had broken them and was afraid to tell anyone.

But she just shook her head, then let her eyes follow Pete as he pushed the manger back.

It finally hit Lydia what was going on.

"Elizabeth, are you not wearing your glasses because you don't think Pete will like you if you wear them?"

The girl snapped her head around to look at her with eyes as big as saucers. "How did you know? Please, don't tell my pa. Or let Pete know."

Lydia smiled as she shook her head and sat down beside Elizabeth on the front of the stage, while

Pete and some of the fathers came to help take down the curtains.

She put her arm around Elizabeth's shoulders.

"Sweetie, if Pete likes you, he likes you for who you are. Not for what you look like. And your glasses are part of who you are now. You're still beautiful and glasses aren't going to take anything away from that."

As she said the words to the girl beside her, she realized she was saying them for herself too. Everything she'd just said applied to her.

Even though she'd never heard Lewis actually say he loved her, she realized she already knew in her heart how he felt. And she wasn't even giving him the chance to decide his future for himself.

Suddenly, she knew exactly what she had to do.

Elizabeth hugged her, then jumped up and went to finish helping. Lydia stood and noticed Lewis and his parents standing with Brooks and Fiona. She finished putting everything away, then went to thank the Reverend for letting her use the church.

After milling around for a while and visiting with each other, everyone finally started to leave. Wishes of Merry Christmas filled the air while each child hugged her tight before heading out the door.

Brooks and Fiona waited by the door for her as she stood by Lewis and his parents.

Her heart suddenly felt like it could be heard in the silence of the room.

"Lydia, I want to apologize again for the horrific display of manners you were witness to yesterday. I assure you, my husband is not the kind of man to be so mean-spirited and hurtful."

She smiled at Anne Kinkaid, who truly was a kind woman. She suspected his father, deep down below the surface of proper society rules and need for appearances, could be a nice man too. He wanted his son home with him and continuing the legacy he'd built.

Turning to face Lawrence, she tilted her head slightly and looked into his eyes. He swallowed hard and averted his eyes to look at Lewis.

"I know you aren't mean, or hurtful, but you should understand how harsh your words can be. And sometimes, they can hurt others. I may not be the perfect woman you'd have chosen for your son. But I assure you, I love him and will do everything I can to keep him happy so he never feels he's given up too much to be with me."

Lewis took her by the arm and turned her to face him. "What are you talking about, Lydia? I've never said anything about not being happy or feeling like I'd be giving anything up to be with you."

She had to smile at the worry in his eyes, when she knew without a doubt he'd never say anything like that.

"No, you didn't. But your father did." She turned

to look at the man whose face was turning a dark shade of red. She didn't know if it was embarrassment or anger but, at this point, she didn't care. It wasn't fair that men like him thought they could control everyone or make decisions that affected other people.

Lewis let his hands drop as he faced his father.

Lawrence shook his head slowly, a smile spreading across his face. "Well, perhaps you should let him know that you accepted money from me. I was merely looking out for your interests, son. And Lydia was more than happy to take the money I gave her to make sure that happened."

Brooks had walked over and was glaring at Lewis's father.

But Lewis was slowly walking toward his father and Lydia was suddenly worried maybe she shouldn't have started any of this. The way he was looking at him, she worried for the older man's safety.

"You tried to pay Lydia to leave me alone? Did you honestly think that I'd just give her up and come home? I'd have spent the rest of my days here trying to convince her that she's the only thing in the world that can make me this happy. And that nothing—and that includes money or prestige—means more to me than her."

"Son, I think you should know. She accepted the money."

Lydia knew how he'd always felt about women in his past who only cared for him for the money. She knew how the words would sound to his ears.

Lewis turned slowly and met her eyes. She prayed he'd see what was in her heart.

Just then, the Reverend walked over from where he'd been in his small back office.

"I wanted to come over and thank you all." He looked at Lydia and she nodded her head toward Lawrence Kinkaid. Turning to face the man, he put his hands out, taking the other man's into a strong handshake.

"Thank you, Mr. Kinkaid for your generous donation to the Kansas Orphanage for Crippled Children."

The look on the man's face almost made her laugh out loud.

Lawrence slowly turned his head to meet her eyes. She shrugged. "You told me to take the money and do what I knew was right in my heart."

He was slowly shaking his head again and this time the smile that emerged covered his face.

"I never thought I'd find anyone who'd stand up to me, especially not when they could've had a lot of money out of the deal."

She reached over to take Lewis's hand and looked up at him. "I'm getting something much more important to me than money. I'd rather have this man in front of me for the rest of my life, than any amount of money you could give me."

Lewis had turned and was pulling her into his arms. "And there's nothing I'd rather do than spend the rest of my life holding you in my arms." He brought his head down slowly and covered her lips in a tender kiss that told her more than any words ever could.

While Brooks blustered in the background to get his hands off his sister and that they were standing in a church, she looked up at Lewis as he pulled back slightly.

His eyes held hers, and he brought his hand up to caress her cheek. "I love you, Lydia. And don't ever doubt how perfect you are in my eyes. There's no one I'd rather hold or nowhere I'd rather be, than with you."

As she stood in the circle of his arms, it was as though the rest of the world had stopped turning. It was just them.

And she knew now that sometimes perfect wasn't always the same for everyone.

But this man holding her was as close to it as she'd ever seen.

EPILOGUE

"The day has gone surprisingly well, considering how many times I was sure my father and your brother would surely come to blows."

They'd spent Christmas Day at the farm with Brooks and Fiona and Lewis's parents had agreed that perhaps they'd come and enjoy a home-cooked meal too. Since last night, Lawrence Kinkaid had done a surprising turnabout-face. In fact, a few times throughout the day, she'd caught him looking at her with the slightest of smiles and he'd always just shake his head in disbelief.

Apparently, it'd been a great deal of money she'd given to the orphanage. He'd been more than generous when giving her that pouch of money and now the orphanage just outside of Abilene would benefit from his donation.

She'd jokingly told Lewis that was her Christmas gift to him.

"Would you like to step outside for a walk?"

They hadn't had much time to be alone today and she'd caught Lewis looking at her many times, a hunger in his eyes that had taken her breath away.

"I'll be keeping my eyes on you, so don't try anything," Brooks grumbled at the table when they announced they were heading out for some fresh air.

Lydia smiled to herself when she saw the glare Fiona sent her husband, letting him know he needed to back off.

Stepping out into the night air, she pulled her jacket tight around her neck. Their breath clouded in the cold air as they started to walk toward the stables. Ruby was standing, tied inside the warmth of the shelter and she smiled as she remembered how gentle the sweet horse had been with her.

As though she sensed Lydia was looking at her, she lifted her head from where she'd been eating and snorted into the air in greeting.

They walked, the snow under their feet crunching while the snowflakes started to fall around them. The sky was lit with stars as far as the eye could see and she was sure she'd never felt more content and full of peace than she did at that moment.

Suddenly, Lewis stopped her, tugging on her

hand and pulling her around to face him. Before she could argue, she was in his arms, tight against him as he grinned down at her.

"I have a present for you." He looked as excited as the children yesterday with the play as he looked at her with eager eyes.

She laughed softly. "You didn't have to give me anything. You've already given me a house, remember?"

They'd announced they were getting married at dinner today and that it would be happening soon. His parents had decided to stay and be witnesses to his marriage, so they planned to do it within the next few days.

"I got this for you a long time ago and never seemed to find the right time to give it to you. It just seemed like so much was happening."

He reached inside his coat pocket, still holding her close in his arms. He pulled something out that was wrapped in soft tissue paper. As she unwrapped it, she glanced up and caught him watching her with a tender smile.

As the paper fell away, she saw the beautiful hair comb she'd admired in the mercantile all those weeks ago. He'd gone back and got it for her.

She choked on a sob, not sure how to thank him for a gift like this. It wasn't the jewels on the comb or how much it had cost. What had touched her heart was that he'd thought to get it for her after hearing her mention she thought it was beautiful.

The gesture of the gift touched her heart. Reaching up, she touched his cheek with her gloved hand and smiled with her whole heart.

"Thank you."

He was still grinning. "So you like it then?"

He knew full well how much she loved it.

She nodded and pressed herself up against him more. "I love it. And I love you. More than you will ever know."

His smile slowly left his face, replaced by the look of pure hunger and longing. Bringing his lips to meet hers, he whispered, "I can't wait to spend the rest of my life letting you show me."

As their lips met, she smiled to herself.

She planned to do just that.

SPECIAL SNEAK PEEK OF PHOEBE'S PROMISE: BOOK ONE IN THE OREGON SKY SERIES

CHAPTER 1

"I don't know how you're going to pull this off, Phoebe. There is no way anyone is going to believe you're a man."

Phoebe clenched her hands tighter on the reins, staring ahead at the scene before her. Everywhere she looked, she saw the white of the covered wagons. Men were walking around, talking, and lifting supplies into the wagons.

There were women, too. But most of the women who would be making the trek across the country were married, many with children hanging from their skirts.

Phoebe watched them closely as they soothed crying babies, shook clothing out of the back of the wagons to get the dust out, and crouched down tending to the meal that would feed their families tonight before the start of their long journey in the morning.

They all wore long dresses covered with aprons and many had bonnets on their heads. Some women had their bonnets hanging off the back of their necks as they worked to ready the wagons.

"Grace, this is what we have to do. Luke wouldn't send us here if he didn't think it would be safe for us. We have to do it; you know there's no other option for us."

She tried to calm her own nerves by soothing her sister's worries but inside, her stomach was in knots, threatening to give her away.

It was hard to believe that just a day ago, her brother Luke had sent them on with the wagon full of supplies to make a trip across the country. He was heading back to St. Louis to deal with their uncle, Ivan, a man they suspected of having a hand in their father's death.

She felt a twinge in her chest as she thought of her pa. He had died heroically during the great fire that had erupted in the city almost a year ago. He'd gone into their burning mercantile to save a baby their uncle had said was still inside.

But after the fire was out, they found no sign of a baby ever having been in there.

Her ma died from cholera just a month before their father's death, so she and Grace were left in the care of their uncle until their brother Luke came home. He'd fought with their father a year before and left, saying he was going looking for gold.

When he finally came home, Phoebe told him her suspicions and let him know her fears about her uncle. He wasted no time getting them away from there.

She tried to keep her anger toward her brother in check. Not only had he left them to deal with the death of their parents alone, while he went on adventures all over the country, but then he wouldn't listen to reason when she tried telling him she could handle her uncle. She wanted to help prove that he'd killed her pa.

Now, here she was sitting on a loaded wagon, about to set off on a trail across the country with only her sister and a bunch of strangers.

Except, of course, for Colton Wallace, the man she had to find. Her brother had sent a letter explaining everything and told her to find him and give it to him. He promised her the man would take care of them.

She didn't have much to go on, other than he was tall, and had dark hair and blue eyes. She figured there were likely a hundred men in their company fitting that description.

"Just sit here with the wagon and I will be right back." She hooked the reins around the front of the wagon. The oxen pawed the ground, then bent their heads to see what grass they could find to graze on.

Her sister grabbed her arm before she could get down from the seat. Phoebe stopped and stared into fearful green eyes. "Please don't be too long!" Her sister pleaded.

Grace was only twelve years old and Phoebe felt terrible leaving her alone for even a moment. She was scared herself and she was six years older.

"I won't be long, I promise." She reached out and patted her sister's hand, trying to offer her some reassurance. All around them, voices were shouting out orders and people were running wild getting everything ready for the trip ahead.

The truth was her own body trembled with fear but she would never let her sister know that. Right now, she was all Grace had to depend on and she wasn't going to let her down. Luke believed in her and she was going to prove his confidence in her wasn't misplaced.

She wasn't used to wearing pants and the boots on her feet were hot and uncomfortable, not to mention a size too big. But in their haste to leave the city, the ill-fitting clothes and boots were all they could find.

She tugged her jacket tighter around her shoulders, not wanting anyone to see her curves even though she had wrapped those same curves so tight with fabric, there wasn't much chance of that happening anyway.

The hat she wore was a bit big but she was at least able to pull her hair up tight beneath it. She knew if anything gave her away, it would be her hair. Someone once told her it was the color of the brightest sunset or as her uncle said, the color of the devil's own eyes.

Luke told her to cut it off but she hadn't been able to do it. Now though, as she glanced around her and saw the reality of her situation, she realized she should have listened to her brother. She couldn't risk getting caught.

Two women alone on a wagon train was too tempting a target for unscrupulous men.

"Hmph! Watch where you're going there, young man! You can get yourself run over if you don't keep your eyes in front of you." A burly man with a grey beard down to his chest bumped into her, almost knocking her over as she came around a wagon.

"Sorry." She tried to keep her voice low, looking toward the ground in an attempt to hide her face.

Walking as quickly as she could, she gripped the letter in her hand tighter. She weaved in and out between wagons, sidestepping scampering, excited children, while narrowly managing to escape being stepped on by an unyoked ox.

Fear kept her moving forward. She needed to find the man her brother had sent her to find. If her brother trusted him, she knew he was someone who'd help her get her sister to safety.

Phoebe spotted a man near a small group of wagons, shouting orders from atop a horse. She stopped to take a better look. Her brother said he could be a bit intimidating in his manners, but he assured her he wasn't half as ornery as he let everyone believe he was. Her brother had been trying to make her feel better but she knew he was also likely trying to warn her about the man she needed to trust.

"Take that wagon and move it over there out of the way! And get those kids out from under our feet before someone gets themselves killed!" The man's voice boomed across the space between the wagons.

The man hopped down, reaching out to pull a small child out of harm's way as a wagon rolled past.

As she watched, the child's mother ran over to take her son from the man. Phoebe couldn't hear what he said to her but she nodded and then practically dragged the child back to their wagon.

Phoebe was so wrapped up in watching the woman and child she nearly jumped from her boots when she noticed the man was now standing right in front of her.

"Where are your parents?" He was scowling at her. She hoped this wasn't Colton Wallace.

Swallowing hard, she lowered her voice to speak.

"Don't have any folks here with me. It's just me and my little sister."

The man raised an eyebrow, then whipped his hat off his head and swept his hair back out of his eyes before slapping it back on his head. She noticed it was in need of a cut and the color was as black as coal. His eyes were bluer than the sky above them.

He had to be the man her brother sent her to find. He didn't look happy to be left in charge of a young man and his sister, so she was sure he'd be even less happy when he discovered the truth.

"Do you realize the extent of the journey we have ahead of us through the roughest stretches of land you will ever see in your life? This isn't going to be a two or three-day ride. So if you think you are going to try doing a trip like this on your own, with a younger sister to take care of, then I question your sanity. I can't tell you no but I can tell you right now I don't have the time or inclination to be spending the entire trip looking after a boy and his sister." His jaw was clenched tight and she could see the muscles in his neck moving as he tried to control his anger.

Lifting her chin a little higher, she thought she saw a flicker of his eyes as he creased his eyebrows and she saw him lean in closer to her. Determined not to back away from his scrutiny, she looked him straight in the eye. "Are you Colton Wallace?"

He didn't move a muscle for what seemed like forever, then slowly he nodded his head. "I am. And, I didn't just fall off the turnip wagon. So do you want to tell me who you are and exactly why you are dressed as a boy?"

Thrusting the letter into his hands, she didn't say a word until he finally lowered his gaze and opened the envelope. She watched him as he read the words her brother had hastily scrawled onto the page. Colton slowly lifted his face, his eyes holding her in place.

Her heart pounded in her chest but she kept her gaze on his, not prepared to back down.

Grabbing her by the arm, he dragged her to a tree off to the side of the gathered wagons.

"Get your hands off me you big oaf!" She was tired, hungry, and just as upset about the situation she found herself in as he was. If he thought he was going to toss her around like a sack of flour, he had another thing coming.

"Quiet!" He stopped and turned to face her again. "Now, do you mind telling me what the hell is going on? If you expect me to believe you are Luke Hamilton's sister and that he wants me to take you all the way across the country with nothing more than a letter telling me so, you had better start talking!"

CHAPTER 2

His nerves were stretched as tight as they could go and he was trying his hardest not to lose his temper. The stress of the day had worn on him as he readied the wagon train to start off in the morning. News like this wasn't welcome at this point.

The moment she lifted her eyes and glared at him, he had known she was a woman and not the boy she was pretending to be. The letter from his friend said he needed Colton to look after his younger sisters until he could join them, hopefully soon. But he hadn't been sure how long he would be and he thought dressing his oldest sister as a boy would help keep her safer on the trail. A young woman without a chaperone was too much temptation for the single men, especially when they appeared as pretty as he suspected she did without the boy clothes.

He noticed her swallow hard and wondered if she'd turn around and run away from him. He almost hoped she would.

"My brother is Luke Hamilton, and he assured me you were someone he would trust with his life." Her eyes flashed with anger. "However, from what I have seen, I'm not sure why he would consider a man as abrasive as you a friend." He heard her voice catch as she spoke and he realized she was trying hard to put on a brave face in a situation that was obviously beyond her control.

Pulling his hat from his head again, he slapped it against his thighs, trying to get his own frustration under control.

He whipped out the letter and reread the words carefully.

COLTON,

I am trusting you with the only remaining family I have, my sisters Phoebe and Grace. I returned from our travels to find my mother dead from cholera and my father killed in a fire. I have my suspicions that it was our uncle who is responsible for his death and I intend to find out the truth.

Since I was gone, my sisters were forced to live with my uncle. He has tried to harm both of them, and I can't have them here while I do what I need to do. I am left with no choice but to get them as far away from him as I can.

I know it is asking a great favour of you to take them with you but I will do everything in my power to join up with you along the way.

If, however, I can't catch up with the train, I am asking you to take them with you to your family in Oregon until I can come for them. I will explain everything then.

Phoebe is tough as nails and she will do her part to get them both to the other end of the trail, with or without my help. I've dressed her as a boy hoping to keep her safe along the way, although I suspect it will be difficult to keep that hidden for the entire journey, which I am sure by that time, you will be able to handle.

There is no one else I would trust with something as precious as my sisters and I am hoping you will do me this favor. I will forever be indebted to you.

Luke

COLTON STARED down at the letter, listening to the sounds of the people milling around, preparing their wagons. Dust settled around him as people and animals moved throughout the camp readying everything for the morning.

"So, why didn't your brother bring you here himself, instead of sending you to me, with only a letter asking me to do something as foolhardy as dragging you two girls across the country with me?"

She crossed her arms in front of her and, by the way she was clenching her jaw, he could tell she was biting her tongue hard to keep from giving away her own frustration. "He said he knew if he came, you would argue and likely wouldn't agree to help. He sent us on our own with a letter knowing you'd be unable to say no." She hadn't even tried to lie.

His eyes fell to the letter in his hands. He had to get his anger under control.

"Well, I don't see any other option. I can't very well leave you sitting here on your own." He lifted his gaze, finding himself caught in her angry stare. Her arms were crossed in front of her and she wasn't moving a muscle. If he didn't know better, she was daring him to say he wouldn't take her.

"I assure you, I'm not thrilled with the prospect of spending the next few weeks traveling all the way across the country, wearing cumbersome clothes that are two sizes too big. I haven't been given any choice in the matter either, my brother practically dragged us here. I tried to assure him I could handle my uncle as I have *already* been doing since my parents died. The only reason I didn't fight him more was because I needed to get my sister away from our uncle." He watched her shoulders hitch as she took a deep breath. "So, if you're worried about me being a burden, I promise you I will do my share of the work and you won't be bothered with me or my sister any more than you would with any of the others in this wagon train."

Colton couldn't take his eyes off hers. He found himself actually believing she could make this trip on her own.

He and Luke Hamilton had been through a great deal together and he knew he'd never betray his friend's trust. But he sure didn't like the thought of having to keep two women safe for the next few months. The risks they'd face as they moved west were more than any of them could imagine.

"So, I'm guessing you are Phoebe?"

She nodded.

"And, what provisions did you bring for the trip? I hope your brother thought to provide for your needs and didn't leave me to do that as well." He was irritated and he knew he sounded like a petulant child but he didn't care.

Phoebe stood completely still in front of him.

"So Mr. Wallace, does that mean you will take us with you?" She appeared relieved even though she didn't seem happy to be here, either. Her face was dirty; there were deep circles under her eyes and she seemed too grown up to be so young. She'd obviously carried a great burden on her shoulders—just getting her and her sister to the wagon train on her own must've taken its toll.

He started walking back toward the wagons.

"Yes. Your brother is a friend so I won't turn my back on his request to help. But I'm not going to like it." He didn't know why added that last bit.

He turned back to find Phoebe trying to keep pace in boots that were too big. He ground his teeth together, willing his anger to calm.

"And, before we leave tomorrow, I'm taking you to the closest mercantile and getting you a pair of boots that fit properly! How did you plan on walking thousands of miles in those boots?"

He turned and started to walk away but before he could move three steps, something hit him square on the shoulder. He reached up to rub the spot where he'd been hit, then looked down to see one of the boots in question lying beside him on the ground.

Slowly, he bent down to pick it up, then turned back to face the woman who was now glaring at him, wearing only one boot. Her hands were in tight fists at her side and her chest was heaving as she breathed.

He raised an eyebrow.

She walked over, calmly took the boot from his hand, put it back on, then walked right past him—as though nothing had just happened.

He suddenly tasted dirt and realized his mouth was hanging open as he watched her walk away. " I am quite sure my brother thought of everything; however, you are welcome to come take a look for yourself." He watched her retreating back and had no choice but to follow her.

Catching up with her, he grabbed her arm and bent low enough that only she could hear his next words. "I am the captain of this wagon train, so you will not do anything like that again. If you do, you will have to face the same consequences as any other who would dare to challenge me. Do I make myself clear?"

She squinted as she returned his gaze. Her eyes brightened when she was angry.

"Perfectly." And with that, she turned and walked away again.

Uh-oh! It looks like Colton just may have met his match in the fiery Phoebe! Don't miss this exciting series!

AVAILABLE FEBRUARY 2022

ABOUT THE AUTHOR

USA Today Bestselling Author, Kay P. Dawson writes sweet western romance – the kind that leaves out all of the juicy details and immerses you in a true, heartfelt love story. Growing up pretending she was Laura Ingalls, she's always had a love for the old west and pioneer times. She believes in true love, and finding your happy ever after.

Happily married mom of two girls, Kay has always taught her children to follow their dreams. And, after a breast cancer diagnosis at the age of 39, she realized it was time to take her own advice. She had always wanted to write a book, and she decided that the someday she was waiting for was now.

She writes western historical, contemporary and time travel romance that all transport the reader to a time or place where true love always finds a way.

www.ingramcontent.com/pod-product-compliance
Lightning Source LLC
La Vergne TN
LVHW030921080826
845145LV00013B/2995

* 9 7 8 1 6 3 9 7 7 2 0 9 4 *